The Girl
in the
Window

A Suspense Novel

Renée Pawlish

ACKNOWLEDGEMENTS

The author gratefully acknowledges all those who helped in the writing of this book, especially: Beth Treat, Janice Horne, and a special shout-out to Tracie Ann Setliff and Donna Thompson. Any mistakes are mine. If I've forgotten anyone, please accept my apologies.

To all my beta readers: I am in your debt!

Maureen Anderson, Bill Baker, Suzanne S. Barnhill, Renee Boomershine, Jean Brown, Wanda Bryant, Gia Cantwell, Irene David, Kate Dionne, Betty Jo English, Tracy Gestewitz, Patti Gross, JoAnn Ice, Kay, Joyce Kahaly, David King, Cindi Knowles, Maxine Lauer, Debbie McNally, Karen Melde, Becky Neilsen, Ann Owen, Janice Paysinger, Charlene Pruett, Fritzi Redgrave, Ian Reid, Chance Rideout, Judith Rogow, Mary Lou Romashko, Bev Smith, Janet Soper, Al Stevens, Ted Stewart, Joyce Stumpff, Morris Sweet, Jennifer Thompson, Patricia Thursby, Georgi Tileston, Jo Trowbridge, Shelly Voss, Lu Wilmot, Marlene Van Metre

The Girl in the Window

CHAPTER ONE

It was the same thing, five days a week.

Caleb McCormick backed out of his driveway in his Mercedes S-class sedan. The car was black and sleek, and it shimmered in the morning light. The engine rumbled and growled, but it was a comforting sound to me, like the purr of a cat – a big cat. It was the perfect car for the perfect man, the man I looked for each morning.

The Mercedes reached the street, turned, and drove slowly past my house. I slid to the side of the window. I didn't want him to see me watching. Not again. But I peeked out anyway.

Caleb McCormick. Thirty-three years old, a financial advisor. His dark hair neatly trimmed, one lost dark curl falling down his forehead in a sexy way. I imagined his blue eyes sparkling as he quickly donned a pair of Oakley sunglasses to ward off the early morning April sun.

Gawd, he's gorgeous.

The Mercedes neared the corner, slowed down and disappeared. I let out a lungful of air I hadn't realized I was holding in. The last time he'd driven by – yesterday morning a little after seven – he'd glanced my way. He'd seen me watching – not for the first time – and waved, a half-smile on his baby face. I'd lifted a hand in return and smiled back. It was our morning connection, a treasured moment. At least for me.

What did he think when he saw me, each weekday morning at the same time, standing in the window in my pink silk robe, staring out at him? It must not have bothered him – after all, he always drove by and acknowledged me in a seemingly pleasant way.

With a sigh, I moved back in front of the window and gazed down the street, where the Mercedes had just been. Then I glanced in the other direction, toward his house, and frowned. After what had happened with his wife yesterday, I needed to be careful.

I drew in another breath, let it out slowly, then turned from the window and plodded back into the kitchen. I poured a cup of coffee and stood at the counter and sipped it. I peered out the window. The back yard needed tending to. Dead leaves lay scattered under bushes and all over my flower beds. A small vegetable garden in the corner needed cleaning out. I usually loved to get out there and get my hands dirty, but I hadn't had any motivation lately. I spent too much time thinking about Caleb.

Why couldn't I have had a husband like that? I pictured Caleb and began fantasizing about what it would be like to have him come home to me. It would be – well, certainly not what I'd had. I was still thinking about him when I saw what time it was. I swore. Kristen was going to be here soon, and I hadn't even dressed yet. What would she think?

I went upstairs, showered, and threw on some makeup. I put on khaki slacks and a white blouse, trying to make myself feel prettier than I felt right now. Just as I was putting on some earrings, the doorbell rang. I dashed back downstairs and opened the front door.

"Amber, you don't need to dress up for me," Kristen Smalls said as she flew past me, down the hall, and into the kitchen.

I'd known Kristen since college. We were sorority sisters, and we'd become fast friends. We'd roomed together, studied together, partied together, and even ended up sharing some of the same guys – not at the same time. She was not only my best friend, she was also my lawyer.

"Get me a cup of coffee before I die," Kristen ordered. She plopped her leather briefcase on the island, pulled out a barstool, and sank into it. "I was up late last night."

"A new man?" I asked as I poured her coffee.

"Hardly. I'm part of that big case, and I have a lot on my plate. And then I needed to get your paperwork finished."

Kristen was a criminal attorney, and she was doing me a favor handling my divorce from my soon-to-be ex, Rick Aldridge.

"Here's where things are with Rick," she said as she dug into her briefcase.

I handed her coffee, then reached into the refrigerator for hazelnut creamer.

"Thanks," she said. She set a file folder on the island, took the creamer and poured a generous amount into her cup. She swished the coffee around, then took a gulp. "Aaah. I wish they could shoot this into my veins."

I forced a laugh and waited for the bad news. She finally looked at me.

"Rick isn't going to give you a cent more than he has to."

"Oh?" I leaned against the counter.

She nodded and sipped her coffee, her brown eyes contemplating me over the rim of the cup. I pursed my lips and shrugged.

"That's it?" she said.

"What do you want me to say?"

"You know you should be asking for more."

"Maybe." I glanced toward the TV in the other room. The *Today* show was on, the sound muted. Matt Lauer was interviewing a celebrity who was in the middle of a nasty divorce. How familiar.

"Amber," Kristen said softly.

I turned back to her. "I don't have the fight in me."

"You're going to need money if you're going to keep this house."

My eyes wandered again, taking in the kitchen with its cherry cabinets, granite countertops, and hardwood floors. Rick and I had moved in eighteen months ago. We'd spent a lot of money to buy this place.

"I thought this was going to be my dream home," I said. "We'd settle down and have kids ..."

Kristen put down her cup. It clinked loudly. She crinkled up her face in her no-nonsense look.

"Sweetie, you know there were problems with Rick, even before that, and moving into this house wasn't going to change anything."

"Yeah, well." I couldn't manage a witty comeback, so I glared at her, but she didn't notice. "Maybe I was naïve, but I thought it would. I figured maybe he'd settle down a little bit."

Kristen stared at me in disbelief, then waved a hand around. "You still want to keep this place? It's awfully big for just one person."

She was right. The main level had a living room with expensive furniture that we'd bought but rarely used, and a dining room where Rick and I had never shared a meal. Only the den had seen activity, mostly Rick watching TV, that is, when he'd been around. Upstairs was a lovely master suite and two more bedrooms, one I'd thought would soon be turned into a nursery. But that never happened. There was plenty of room in the basement as well. Rick could've enjoyed his man cave, the escape from a passel of kids. The truth was, he'd hardly gone down there, and now it was just a big empty space because *I* didn't have anything to fill it with. But I wasn't ready to give this house up just yet. My mind flashed to Caleb McCormick.

"There could still be a man in my life. Hell, I'm only thirty-two, don't say my life's over."

Kristen laughed. "I'm not saying that. But if Rick continues to fight you like he is now, you're going to have to get a job to pay the mortgage if you want to stay here."

"I haven't had a job in a while."

"You still have skills. Don't sell yourself short."

"The problem is, I don't want to work."

Kristen tapped the countertop with a manicured fingernail. She looked every bit the power attorney in her tailored blue suit, her blond hair falling stylishly around her shoulders, those brown eyes boring into me.

"I know Rick's leaving has been hard on you," she said. "You didn't see it coming."

I was grateful she didn't tack on, *although you should have.*

"How much do you have in savings?" she went on.

"It's going to run out in a few months."

The tapping grew more intense. "You need to act now."

"I know."

She glanced around again. "You wanted to be in this neighborhood where the husbands have their great careers and the women stay home and eat bon-bons."

"Bon-bons," I smirked. "That's not what happens."

"How many times have I heard you talk about that woman across the street, what's her name?"

"Erin," I said with a hint of bitterness in my tone.

Caleb's wife.

"See? Even the way you say her name. You don't like these women with their country-club lifestyles and their expensive cars and clothes. It's not you, no matter how much you try to sell it to yourself. You had a great career, and I don't know why you gave it up."

Not to brag, but I'd been a really good software engineer and had been moving up in a big company before I'd met Rick, gotten married, and quit my job. But the career hadn't been what I'd wanted. Or what I thought I'd wanted.

"Erin's fine," I said, avoiding Kristen's other thoughts.

"You told me she's given you the cold shoulder from the moment you moved into this house."

"Maybe."

"Or is it because she knows you have the hots for her husband?"

I felt my cheeks burning. "What do you mean?"

"Come on. You can't fool me. You think he's something special."

"Well ... he is ..." My voice trailed off.

"Gorgeous."

I grinned. "Yeah."

"Of course he is. But he's married."

"I know that."

Kristen stared at me. "You remember when I was here a few weeks ago? Caleb came home from work while you and I were talking in the driveway. I saw how you looked at him. And I've heard how you talk about him. He's got the perfect job, and the great house, and the flawless wife. The next thing you'll know, Erin will be popping out kids and they'll have the perfect family."

"I'd kill for a life like that," I said, then let out a mirthless laugh.

"It's not going to happen, at least not with Rick." She pushed the papers across the island. "Read that when you have a minute and let me know what you think. I've tried to come up with something fair for you."

I didn't even look at the papers. "Just give him what he wants."

"That's not a good idea. This is your lawyer speaking as much as your friend."

"I don't have the fight in me."

She frowned. "I'm not sure you ever did."

"So?"

Her eyes softened. "It's got to be hard for you, with everything that Rick did." She hesitated. "You're vulnerable right now."

"And?"

"Don't do anything stupid." She picked up her cup, gulped down more coffee, and stood up. "I've got to get to the office."

She grabbed her briefcase and quickly headed down the hall to the front door. I had to hurry to catch up. She yanked open the door, then spun around and gave me a quick hug.

"Hang in there. And don't do anything stupid," she repeated.

I laughed. "I'll be fine."

"I know you think this was the textbook life for you, because of your mom and all, but …"

"I know, we've had this talk before."

"You haven't been in this house that long. Are you sure you want to stay?"

"I don't know."

She nodded. "Rick's lawyer has been bugging me, so listen. Whatever you do, don't sign anything that Rick or his lawyer sends your way."

"I won't."

Then she was out the door in a cloud of perfume-scented air. I followed her out. She hurried to her Lexus and drove off with a squeal of tires. Kristen, always in a rush. So unlike what went on around me.

I stepped off the porch and looked down the street. All the houses looked beautiful, the yards blooming with spring flowers, the grass finally greening up after a long winter. No matter what Kristen said, it still seemed like the perfect neighborhood to me.

The garage door of a house down the street slowly opened and I watched as Erin McCormick backed her red BMW out of the driveway.

CHAPTER TWO

I backpedaled and almost tripped on the porch steps in my haste to get back into the house. I shut the storm door and stood back as the Beemer pulled up to the house across the street. Erin was wearing a pink cap and sunglasses.

The garage door opened and Melissa Lowenstein emerged, a golf bag slung over her shoulder. She and Erin and Tiffany Caruthers, the neighbor directly across the street from me, were all good friends. But none of them was fond of me. I tried to fool myself that I didn't know why, but I did. They knew how I felt about Caleb.

Melissa punched numbers in a keypad by the garage door and it slowly closed. Then she walked down the driveway in her white skirt, yellow shirt, and white visor. Erin popped the trunk and Melissa put her golf bag in. She took a moment to adjust her visor and hopped in the passenger side, and the Beemer raced down the street. Just as Kristen had said. The neighborhood wives off for their day at the club while their husbands were off at work.

I went back into the kitchen, dumped out the coffee cups, and put them in the dishwasher. That would probably be the most exciting thing I did all day. I looked out at my neglected yard, shrugged, and turned away from the window. I ignored the papers from Kristen, plodded into the den and watched the end of the *Today* show and then some other talk show. That turned into some soap I didn't even know.

I finally got up and looked at the paperwork Kristen had left. She'd drafted an agreement that would give me maintenance – what used to be called alimony – for four years. It would leave me with enough to live in the house and pay the bills. I certainly couldn't live here forever on that, but it would keep me going for a while. I stared at the papers. She'd said Rick would fight it, and I wondered where that would lead. Did I have it in me to go after this?

Kristen had taped a yellow Sticky-note to the last page, saying to call her once I'd read everything. *She was busy now*, I said to myself, finding the excuse not to. I set the papers down and fixed some lunch – a salad with tomatoes and deli chicken – but I hardly tasted it. I put every-thing away and stood for a long time at the kitchen sink, staring into the back yard. Then I heard my neighbor Kayla.

She'd had her first baby a little over a year ago, a little girl named Talon. For crying out loud, where had they come up with that name? I leaned over the sink and craned my neck to see over the fence. Kayla had Talon in a little swing, and Talon was giggling and clapping her hands. Kayla's face was aglow, and the scene made my heart ache. I went back into the den and cranked up the volume on the TV.

I had no idea what I watched the rest of the afternoon. Finally, around six, I pushed myself out of the chair and went to get the mail. John Caruthers – Tiffany's husband – was also getting his mail. He was in a suit, his tie loosened, a polished, casual ease about him. I waved and he held up a hand, then strode up his driveway and into the house. I didn't know him very well, had only talked to him a time or two when Rick and I'd first moved into the neighborhood. Seeing him while we got our mail was the extent of our interaction.

I went back inside and resumed watching TV. Shadows crossed the room before I finally got up and fixed a drink. I'd never been one for heavy drinking, and I wasn't going to make it a habit now, but at the moment, a stiff drink seemed better than dinner. I sat at a small table in the breakfast nook and watched darkness creep into the back yard. Night finally consumed the house. The vodka didn't sit well on my empty stomach, so I had some crackers and went upstairs.

My cell phone rang around nine. It was Kristen. I hadn't thought to call her after she got off work, and I didn't pick up now. A moment later, chimes sounded. She'd left a voicemail. I listened to it.

"Did you read the paperwork?" she asked. "Do it and call me back. We need to be in control of the situation, not Rick. Come on, sweetie. Buck up."

Her type of tough love.

I turned off the phone, soaked in a hot bath, and went to bed.

***

The next morning, I was up early. Caleb left for work a little after seven, as usual, and I was in the front window in my robe, watching. He looked good today. He might've gotten a haircut. He smiled and we waved at each other, and then he was gone.

I stood for the longest time, staring out the window. Then the red Beemer backed out of the McCormick driveway. Erin wasn't wearing her golf cap today. She was probably going to the health club. Keep the figure, that was important. A hand went to my waist. Were my muscles turning to flab? I should've been working out, but I couldn't remember the last time I'd gone to the health club. Like the yard, something else I'd neglected. Maybe I should start anew and go to the club today. It sounded like such work.

The Beemer headed my way and Erin glanced in my direction, a frown on her face. I shriveled away from the window. I don't know if she saw me or not.

I walked into the kitchen for coffee, then turned on the TV. I sat down for the rest of the *Today* show. Suddenly the doorbell rang, and I wondered who would bother me so early in the morning. As I went through the kitchen, I saw the clock and realized it was after noon. I glanced down. I was still in my robe. I raked a hand through my hair, smoothed the front of the robe, and cinched the belt a little tighter as I walked down the hall and opened the door.

A tall man in a light gray suit with a white shirt and no tie stood on the porch. He had curly brown hair and brown eyes that I had once thought were devastatingly alluring, but now appeared cold and harsh.

"Hello, Rick."

"We need to talk."

He pushed past me and into the house. He nearly toppled a tall crystal vase that sat on a slender table in the foyer as he stomped into the kitchen. I righted the vase, briefly wondering why I kept it. He'd given it to me as a wedding gift, and it was expensive. But did it matter now? I thought as I quickly followed him.

He grabbed a glass from a cupboard by the sink and filled it with tap water. He still knew where everything was, even though he hadn't been here in six months. I had a fleeting thought of what he might've done if I'd rearranged things since he moved out. Then I realized he knew I'd never do something like that. I was too routine. I leaned against the wall near the entryway and stared at his back. He drained the glass and set it on the counter, then turned around to face me.

"Look at you," he said. "It's lunchtime and you aren't even dressed."

My hand started to primp my hair, but I stopped. "How's work?"

"It's just fine." He reached into his coat pocket and pulled out some folded papers. "Your lawyer – Kristen – hasn't gotten back to me, and you haven't answered any of my calls or emails." He held up the papers dramatically. "This is what *my* lawyer has come up with. You need to sign them."

I was tempted to grab the papers and do exactly that, but Kristen's voice hammered in my ears, saying don't do anything or sign anything until I consulted with her. And for once I heeded that. I slowly shook my head.

"I can't sign anything until I let Kristen see it."

He swore, then stepped up to the island and slapped the papers down.

"Look, you've been dragging this out for months. I wanted to make a clean break and move on, but you won't do anything."

I looked at him for a long time. "Kristen said you don't want to give me anything."

"Why should I?" he snapped. "I've worked hard on my career. You used to work hard at yours. Why should I give you something now when you're perfectly capable of going back to work? You don't need this house or anything in it."

I shrugged. "Why are you doing this to me? After everything that happened."

"Because I can. Because you don't have a spine. You don't fight back." He sucked in a breath, his nostrils flaring. "Just because you want to wallow in self-pity and don't want to do anything doesn't mean I should have to pay for it."

"Maybe you should," I whispered.

He glared at me, then put his index finger on the papers. "Sign this so we can move on. Do you hear me?"

I stared at him. He came around the island and moved close to me. His Paco Rabanne cologne was spicy and masculine, and I had a flashback to when I'd first met him. He'd smelled so good. He raised a hand, and I was suddenly back in the present. I thought he might hit me. Then he put his hand gently on my shoulder.

"I'm sorry things didn't work out. But you need to get on with your life, like I have."

"Oh, you have?"

"Don't do this."

He looked at me, and the pity in his eyes made me wince. Then he walked down the hall and out the front door. I went to the living room window, and stood and watched as he got into his dark blue Lexus and pulled out of the driveway. He drove down the street, but slowed because Erin was walking along the sidewalk. The Lexus stopped and Erin gave him a tentative smile. She stepped into the street and up to the Lexus. She put her elbow casually on top of the car and talked to Rick for a minute as if they were old friends. But then her lips formed a thin line, and her eyes narrowed. She shook her head angrily as she jabbed a finger at Rick, then finally moved back to the sidewalk. I couldn't tell what Rick said to her before he drove away. I'd been watching Rick's car, but when I turned back to Erin, she was looking in my direction. I didn't know if she could see me, but she was scowling. Then she spun around, walked across her lawn, and disappeared inside her house.

I finally moved away from the window and trudged back into the kitchen. I stared at the papers that Rick had left. They were sitting by the documents that Kristen had given me. I didn't read any of them, but shuffled back into the den. Kristen called later, but I let it go to voice-mail. I didn't bother listening to it.

That night, I listened to the ten o'clock news while I got ready for bed, then stood in the dark and looked out my bedroom window. Some lights were on in other houses. I often wondered what the neighbors were doing. My next-door neighbor Kayla and her husband – I couldn't even remember his name – were probably in bed, exhausted, and grateful for a little rest while Talon was asleep. What about Melissa and her husband Bill? Their lights were still on. Were they watching the late shows?

I gazed down the block. Caleb and Erin's house was dark. I'd seen their Mercedes leaving earlier. Had they gone for a nice dinner, and now were they back, a little boozed up and feeling amorous? Was Caleb making love to Erin right now, softly, tenderly, in a way Rick rarely had with me? I bit my lip.

Farther down the street, a dark sedan was parked at the curb. It looked a little like Rick's blue Lexus. I stared at it, but couldn't be sure. I couldn't imagine him caring enough to spy on me. Had I seen that car there some other night recently? A dark thought entered my mind. Was Rick seeing someone else in the neighborhood? I pictured him earlier today, talking to Erin.

I shuddered. If Rick and Erin were screwing around, that would sure ruin the picture I'd had of Erin and Caleb at home having beautiful, candle-lit, romantic sex. If so, that would ruin the passionate activities I'd pictured Erin and *Caleb* in.

Then I shook my head. Erin would never have an affair and hurt Caleb. They were madly in love, and everyone in the neighborhood knew it. I sometimes wished that was different, that they'd divorce and Caleb could be with me. But that was wishful dreaming.

I continued to watch the car. I could be mistaken. It probably wasn't Rick's. Maybe a neighbor had visitors, or was having a small party. It seemed a little late for a weeknight, but then, most people led more exciting lives than I did. I finally fell into bed, thinking of all those lives around me. Those perfect lives.

***

A week passed. Life went on. All the documents still sat on the counter. I'd finally returned Kristen's call and told her that Rick had dropped off his own paperwork. She told me in no uncertain terms to let her see it first, and not to sign it. I said I wouldn't, but to give me a little more time. She hadn't been happy, but she gave me my space. Rick called, too, and wanted me to sign. I didn't call him back.

I watched the comings and goings of my neighbors. The dark sedan was sometimes parked down the street. Someone must've been visiting one of my neighbors, staying late. Caleb left for work every weekday morning, smiling and waving at me. If only I felt any joy in my returning smile.

The days passed slowly, and I yearned for night, only to lie awake in the dark. On that Sunday evening, I went to bed and stared at the ceiling. The room was dark and still. Lightning flashed, momentarily filling the room with light. Then thunder rumbled, shaking the windows. Rain hit the house, a soft, steady sound. Around midnight, lights from a car pierced through the window. Headlights. Who was coming home? I didn't hear a car, but it was someone nearby. Melissa and Bill? I closed my eyes, willing sleep to come. But it didn't.

Then more headlights, and the growl of an engine. I knew that sound well. Caleb. He and Erin must've gone out, but it was awfully late for them to be coming home. Perhaps they'd been to dinner, and maybe a play or concert. I sighed, wishing I'd been out having a fun evening. The light vanished, and I was left alone, in the dark. I finally fell asleep.

The next morning, I was awake early. I tried to sleep more, but couldn't, so I went downstairs and was at the window a little after seven, waiting. The work week was starting, and Caleb would be driving by any moment.

CHAPTER THREE

It was past 7:20, about the time that Caleb usually drove by. I watched the street. 7:30 came and went. He was running late. He never ran late. Never. I don't know why, but I hadn't looked up the street toward the McCormick house. I finally did. A dark, four-door sedan sat parked at the curb. But this wasn't the one I'd seen parked there before. This one had the distinct look of an unmarked police car.

I glanced up and down the block. No one else was out. I pursed my lips. No matter what was going on, I knew I couldn't go over to the McCormick house and ask. Not only did I not want to interrupt anything, but Erin wouldn't want to talk to me at all.

I watched for a little while longer, and began to worry. What was going on? A hand went to my mouth. Had something happened to Caleb? I started to head out the front door, then realized I hadn't gotten dressed. I ran upstairs, pulled on jeans and a tee shirt, and ran a brush through my hair. That would have to do. I dashed back downstairs and out the front door, then stopped short.

Melissa Lowenstein was standing on the sidewalk across the street, along with Tiffany Caruthers. Melissa was crying. Tiffany nodded and put her arms around Melissa.

My heart thudded in my chest. Something had happened to Caleb,

I was sure of it.

They broke the embrace, and Melissa looked up, her eyes locking with mine. Even at this distance, I felt the ice in her gaze. Then the two women went up the sidewalk and disappeared into Tiffany's house. I felt rocks in the pit of my stomach.

I dashed across my driveway next door to Kayla's house. I hurried up onto the porch and reached to ring the bell, then thought maybe the baby would be asleep. So I tapped lightly on the door. A moment later it opened. Kayla, in yoga pants and a gray tee shirt, was holding Talon on one hip. Talon was playing with a pacifier in her mouth.

"Hi, Amber."

Kayla's voice was sweet and pleasant. She was one of the friendlier women in the neighborhood, and we got along okay. She'd been sensitive to the fact that I'd wanted to have children, and she was actually kind to me when Rick left.

I gestured down the street. "I think something might be happening at the McCormick house. There's a car, well, it looks like a police car, in front of their house."

"Really?" She craned her neck to see past me.

"And I saw Melissa and Tiffany a few minutes ago. They seemed upset about something."

"Oh? I've been busy with Talon, and I haven't been out at all this morning."

"Caleb always leaves for work by 7:30, but I don't think he went in today."

I immediately regretted coming over. I sounded like a snooping neighbor, and I shouldn't have known Caleb's schedule so precisely.

"I see," she said. "I've got to change Talon's diaper first, but then

I'll call Melissa and Tiffany to see what's going on."

"Okay, thanks."

I hurried back to my house, embarrassed by my behavior. And yet something wasn't right. That was a police car at the McCormick house. I was tempted to go across the street and talk to Melissa and Tiffany myself, but I knew they'd give me the cold shoulder. I went inside and stood in front of the living room window. The sedan remained outside the McCormick house. Minutes ticked by. My phone rang and I snatched it up.

"Kayla?"

"No, stranger, it's Mother."

"Oh," I said. "Hi, Mom. What's going on?"

"I haven't talked to you in a while."

"I've been ... busy."

"Doing what?"

I scrambled for words. "I've been looking for a job."

She probably figured I was lying, and I didn't care.

"I don't understand why you don't patch things up with Rick. He's a good man, with a good job."

"Kind of like you did with Dad?" It was pointed, but didn't appear to bother her.

"There's nothing wrong with keeping a man around. Your father and I have done just fine."

"Sure."

"I've always said you can marry poor or you can marry rich." Her voice was smooth and cultured, something practiced. "You married rich, but you didn't hang onto him."

"He wasn't that rich."

"Give it time."

She began prattling on about her and my father, and how great their marriage was. It had seemed that way to me, for a long time. But sometime recently, I realized that hadn't been the case. It wasn't that he abused her in any way, or her him. But there hadn't been a lot of love. It was about money and status. I'd thought I wanted that something. I'd worked only until I found someone who could give me what my father had given my mother. And look where it had gotten me.

The neighborhood was still as I listened to her talk on. She was in so many ways the submissive wife. She did what my father asked, she ran the house, and looked great as she stood by his side. But she was getting what she wanted out of the marriage, too. She had the lifestyle to prove it. I glanced around. Did I want to keep all this? Did I want Rick around again? What would we be like in forty years?

"So anyway, I think you should think about that," she was saying.

My phone beeped and I glanced at the number. Kayla.

"I've got to go, Mom," I said quickly. "I'll call you later."

"All right. Think about what I said, okay? Don't make any rash decisions about the divorce."

How could I be rash when I'd been keeping Rick in suspense for months? I thought.

"I won't," I said. "Bye."

I switched the call.

"Hey, Kayla, what'd you–"

That's as far as I got before she said, "Erin's dead."

CHAPTER FOUR

"What?"

I was stunned, and yet I felt a wave of relief that it wasn't Caleb.

"Erin's dead," she repeated.

"What happened?"

"Her body was found near a dumpster over on Colfax."

"Was she murdered?"

"I don't know."

"What part of town?"

"East of Sheridan, where those skanky motels are."

My hands were clammy. I knew exactly the motels she was talking about. There were a lot of sleazy motels on Colfax Avenue, the kind where you paid by the hour, not the night. Rick had been to one of those motels a couple of years ago. I didn't want to think about that.

"What was Erin doing there?" I asked.

"I don't know anything. I called Melissa and she said that Caleb had called Tiffany last night and said that Erin hadn't come home, and asked if she knew anything. Of course Tiffany didn't, and she couldn't get an answer on Erin's cell. When Tiffany got up this morning, she saw the car out front and called Erin's cell again, but still didn't get an answer. So she tried the McCormick house. Caleb answered and said that

Erin was dead, and that the police were there. He said he'd talk to her later and hung up."

"Poor Caleb," I said.

"I don't understand it. This kind of stuff doesn't happen in a neighborhood like this. Everyone's happy and they get along. Why would anyone want to hurt Erin?"

Everyone got along. Right.

"I know," was all I could say.

"Is the police car still out there?" she asked.

"Yeah."

I immediately regretted saying that, realizing that once again, I sounded like the nosy neighbor. But what better time than now to be spying?

The sudden wail of a baby cut through the phone.

"Talon's crying," she said. "I've got to go. I'll talk to you later."

"Thanks for letting me know about Erin."

"Sure. I just can't believe it."

She ended the call and I stood for a moment, staring at the unmarked police car down the street. Erin. Dead. I again found myself grateful that Caleb was all right.

I finally went into my office across the hall, opened up my laptop, and logged onto the Internet. I googled "Erin McCormick," but all that came up were a Facebook page and some other social media accounts. I tried a different search by using "woman's body" and "Colfax Avenue," but still found nothing. Maybe it was too early for her death to hit the news. Or maybe one stranger's death in a city as big as Denver wasn't newsworthy enough. I had no idea how she'd died, or whether it was murder. I didn't want to think why she'd been at that sleazy motel.

Although I couldn't think what else it might be, given that she was found in an alley.

I went back to the living room and looked out the window again. The unmarked car was still there. I began to pace, not sure what to do. I was dying to go over and talk to Caleb, but I wasn't going to interrupt while the police were there. Time ticked by. I stayed where I was, then fretted over what to do. A long time later, two people came out of the house next door to Caleb's – Tiffany Caruthers' house. One was a tall, bald man, the other a short, stocky woman with shoulder-length brown hair. Both wore dark sunglasses, even though it was overcast. They must've finished talking with Caleb and now were seeing what the neighbors knew. They had to be homicide cops.

They strolled down the walk, both tight-lipped, until they reached Melissa Lowenstein's house. The woman punched the doorbell with purpose. As they waited, I could see a bulge under the woman's blazer, where her gun was holstered. A second later, Melissa opened the door. She'd been waiting for them. She was upset, her head shaking back and forth. The two cops disappeared inside.

They're going to talk to everyone they can find, I thought. How long would it take them to get to me?

I glanced at myself, and made sure I was presentable. Since I didn't go to work or the health club – or anywhere else – I found I'd let myself go a bit. Who was I kidding? It wasn't just that. Rick wasn't around to impress. And at the end, even when he was here, I hadn't cared. Too late now.

Wasn't that a funny thing, though, needing to look good for the cops.

I turned to head upstairs and I saw movement out of the corner of my eye. Tiffany Caruthers had come out of her house. She stood for a moment on her front porch and glanced at Melissa's house. Then she cut across her driveway, through the lawn, and up to the McCormick front door. She tapped on the door, primped her hair, and looked around again. I backed up, even though I was sure she couldn't see me in the window. The door opened and I caught a glimpse of Caleb, and then Tiffany was walking inside. The door shut, and the street was again quiet.

I stared at the McCormick house. I wished I could have been the first one to talk to Caleb, to offer him comfort. Tiffany didn't care about him like I did. She wouldn't know what to say.

A while later, the cops came out of Melissa's house. Just as I'd done when I didn't want Erin or Caleb to see me, I ducked to the side of the window and peeked out. The cops tried the house next to Melissa's. No one was home, so they crossed the street and went up to Kayla's house. I figured it wouldn't be long before they were at my door.

I dashed upstairs and fussed a little over my appearance, putting on a touch of eyeliner and blusher, then hurried back downstairs. I went into the kitchen and poured a cup of coffee, then realized it had been sitting too long and was too strong and bitter. I dumped the coffee and stood looking out the kitchen window, not sure what to do with myself. The doorbell rang and I jumped. I sucked in a deep breath, then went to the door and opened it.

"Are you Amber Aldridge?" the policewoman asked.

"Yes."

"I'm Detective Maddow, and this is Detective Kowalski."

She flashed a badge, then pointed to her partner. He nodded, and I saw my reflection in his dark sunglasses. Did I look nervous?

"Have you heard the news about Erin McCormick?" Maddow

asked.

I nodded. "Yes, I did. I'm shocked."

Maddow stared at me. "Would you have a few minutes to talk to us?"

"Of course." I stepped back. "Come in."

I opened the door wider and gestured toward the living room. They stepped past me and Maddow perched on the edge of the couch, but Kowalksi stood in the doorway. He took off his sunglasses as I moved carefully past him and sat in a wingback chair across from Maddow. She stared at me for a moment, her eyes narrow.

"What happened to Erin?" I asked.

They glanced at each other, and then Maddow took the lead. "She didn't come home last night. Her husband didn't know where she was. He called the police, but you have to wait twenty-four hours before filing a missing persons report. By the time he called back this morning, a delivery man had found her body close to a dumpster near the Standard Motel."

"What was she doing there?"

She ignored that. "When was the last time you saw Mrs. McCormick?"

I thought for a moment. "Yesterday morning. I saw her driving down the street. I think she was going to the health club."

Maddow's eyes were intent. "How do you know that?"

I felt heat on my face and knew I was turning red. "I guess I just assumed that. Erin likes to golf and she likes to go to the health club."

"Are you friends with her?"

I hesitated, then barely shook my head. "We're neighbors."

Kowalski crossed his arms but stayed silent.

"But not necessarily friends," Maddow went on.

"No, I guess not. I don't really socialize with her."

"Why not?"

"I just knew her in the neighborhood, but we didn't really connect." I gnawed my lip. "We ... I haven't lived here that long, and I'm going through a divorce, and that's kept me from getting out much."

"Have you connected with anyone in the neighborhood?"

The burning in my cheeks grew more intense. "Not particularly. Kayla – next door – she and I are friends."

"So you didn't know Erin well," Maddow said.

"I guess not."

"You don't know what she might've been doing in that area by the Standard Motel?" she repeated what I'd asked her earlier.

"I don't have any idea."

I wondered if my voice sounded guilty, as if I knew more about that area and that motel than I should have. But if Maddow or Kowalski detected anything from me, they didn't show it.

"So you saw Erin yesterday morning," she said.

"That's correct."

"Did you see her come home?"

I thought about it. "No, I didn't. Where was her car found?"

"A block over from the motel, in a shopping center parking lot." She stared at me. "Do you usually pay attention to the comings and goings of your neighbors?"

I wanted to disappear into my chair. "Well, no, not necessarily."

"Mr. McCormick says he usually sees you looking out the window in the mornings when he goes to work."

"That's true," I said softly.

"Do you work?"

"Not since I got married."

Maddow stared at me. "You tend to know the routines of the McCormicks."

"I suppose."

"But you have no idea what Erin was up to yesterday."

I shook my head. "As I said, no."

I wasn't sure why she was pestering me with that question again, and I clamped my mouth shut.

"Did you ever see Erin with any strangers, either here in the neighborhood or possibly at the health club or the country club?"

"I haven't been to the health club or the country club in a long time," I said, then realized I hadn't fully answered her question. "No, I haven't seen her with anyone, other than Melissa and Tiffany. And Caleb, of course."

I'd seen her talking to Rick last week, but I left that unsaid.

Detective Kowalski was gazing at me, and it made me uncomfortable. I glanced between them.

"Did you see Caleb yesterday?" Maddow asked.

I nodded slowly. "Going to work, and coming home."

"What about the rest of the evening?"

"No."

She pursed her lips.

"How did Erin die?" I asked.

Maddow looked at me for a long time, then said, "She was hit on the head with a blunt instrument, and it crushed her skull."

I let out a slow breath. "That's awful."

Neither one said anything to that.

"Did you like Erin?" Maddow asked.

"Sure." I wasn't convincing.

"But you didn't socialize with her or her husband? Have them over for dinner, or go over to their house?"

I shook my head. "My husband ... my ex ... soon-to-be ex ... didn't." I didn't know why I was stumbling over my words.

Maddow nodded. "The other neighbors seem very fond of Erin."

"Yes, I'm sure she was nice."

"But you don't know."

"I ... yes, she was nice. I just don't – didn't – know Erin as well as they did."

Maddow continued to study me. "I see. Are you aware of any problems between Erin and her husband?"

I immediately realized why she was asking the question. As her husband, Caleb would automatically be a suspect.

"No," I said truthfully. "As far as I knew, they had a great marriage and they were very much in love. Did you hear differently from somebody?"

Maddow didn't answer that.

"Caleb is always nice to Erin. Was." I suddenly got choked up. Oh, he must be a wreck!

"I think we've bothered you enough," Maddow announced. She stood up and pulled a business card from her pocket. "This has my number on it. If you think of anything that might shed light on what happened to Erin, please give me a call."

I took the card and glanced at Kowalski. He'd donned his sunglasses, and his face remained impassive. He hadn't said a word, and I was curious about what his voice sounded like. I walked them to the door and waited as they walked down the street. I stood at the side of the window and watched as they visited a few other houses. At some point, Tiffany Caruthers emerged from Caleb's house and walked slowly back to hers. She never looked in my direction. The detectives finally returned to their car. Maddow glanced toward my house, then got in, and they drove off.

I went into the kitchen and put Maddow's card in the drawer of a built-in desk. I stood there, numb. Minutes ticked by, and then I decided I couldn't wait any longer. I checked myself in the mirror and walked out my front door.

CHAPTER FIVE

The April sun was behind a thin veil of clouds as I crossed the empty street. I glanced toward Melissa's house, then Tiffany's, but I didn't see either one of them. I doubted they stood in their windows watching the world outside as I did.

As I walked up the sidewalk to the McCormick front porch, my pulse sounded loud in my ears, and I felt a heaviness over me, a feeling of dread. But with that dread also came a sense of anticipation. I didn't really know Caleb very well.

Rick and I had talked to Caleb, when we'd see him on the street, or at the occasional neighborhood barbecue. I realized that I liked Caleb, but I wasn't particularly fond of Erin. And she didn't appear to like me, either. I guiltily wondered whether it had been because of my reaction to Caleb.

I thought back to the first time I'd met him. Rick and I had been outside, helping to unload our moving truck. I was in shorts and a tank top, and I remember I'd been hot and sweaty. Caleb and Erin had come across the street to introduce themselves. He was gorgeous, and I couldn't stop smiling at him. Erin had given me a funny look as we'd talked.

Weeks later, Rick and I had them over for a get-to-know-you

barbecue. It had seemed to go fine. It's funny, I couldn't remember what Erin had been wearing, but Caleb had been in khaki shorts and a tee shirt that said "Cayman Islands" on it. I'd been to Grand Cayman and he and I talked about it, the great snorkeling and the beautiful water. He'd looked so casual and comfortable in his attire that day, and yet he'd looked so sexy. After we'd gotten drinks, I'd watched Caleb and Rick as they cooked steaks on the grill. Now that I think back on it, Erin had been a tad cool to me that day. I'm sure she was aware of my interest in her husband.

I could picture that day as if it were a movie, with Caleb sitting next to me at the picnic table. I'd laughed at all his jokes, a perpetual smile on my face. I wouldn't doubt that I'd batted my eyelashes like a romantic fool. Even Rick had cocked an eyebrow at my behavior. I didn't normally act that way. I flashed on what Kristen had recently said about my marriage having problems long before Rick had actually left. I should've clued in to my behavior with Caleb, and how I'd enjoyed his company more than Rick's.

And had there been something from Caleb? Had he been interested in me? I shook my head. No, that was wishful thinking. Caleb had been so in love with Erin. Even though I'd been laughing at his jokes – flirting with him – he'd gaze adoringly at her.

The McCormicks had never come over for dinner again. When I'd invited them, Erin had one excuse or another. And we hadn't been asked to their house at all. I'd see Caleb outside and I'd say hello, but it seemed like Erin would magically appear and interrupt us, and keep us from talking long. She'd never appeared happy with me. Now that I thought about it, I couldn't blame her…

As I stood on the porch, I hesitated. Now Erin was gone, and so was Rick. Would the situation between Caleb and me change? Could there be something between us now? Just as quickly, I chided myself. How could I think about making a move on him right after his wife had died?

"You really are a schmuck," I whispered to myself.

And yet a part of me was excited at the thought of our being together.

I finally rang the bell. It took a long time, but Caleb finally answered. He was in jeans and a wrinkled blue shirt, his face drawn. Dark crescents ringed his eyes, but he forced a smile.

"Hi, Amber," he said.

"I heard about Erin," I said, then thought he must've known that, but he was too polite to point that out.

"Why don't you come in?"

He stepped back and let me into the foyer. I'd never been into his house, but the layout appeared similar to mine. To the right was an office, the shelves full of books, and to the left was a living room. Down the hall was the kitchen. He gestured toward the kitchen.

"Do you want something to drink?"

I shook my head. "No, I'm fine."

"Come in here."

He showed me into the living room, his aftershave a sweet scent lingering in the air. The furniture and walls were white and antiseptic, just how I would've pictured Erin's home. I sat on a couch that had to be worth several thousand dollars, but was terribly uncomfortable. He sank into a loveseat across from me and stared off into space.

I waited for a moment, then finally said, "I talked to the police."

He nodded.

"They told me very little." I gave him a sympathetic smile. "Do you want to talk about it more?"

He bit his lip, then slowly began. "Erin didn't come home yesterday. I got home from work and she wasn't here. She usually leaves a note or calls or texts me and tells me where she is, but this time she didn't. That was unusual. I called and texted her, but she didn't reply." He frowned. "I was a little worried, but every once in a while something like that happened. She'd get involved in one thing or another and she'd forget to call, and her phone would be on vibrate and she wouldn't notice when I tried to get in touch with her. But last night was different. She was never gone this long. It got dark and she still wasn't home. Finally, around ten, I called Tiffany and Melissa, but neither one had heard from her. They both tried to call her, but she didn't answer. Then I called the police, but they said they couldn't do much. They asked if I'd called the hospitals, which I hadn't, and they said they couldn't fill out a missing persons report unless she'd actually been missing for at least twenty-four hours. So I hung up and called the hospitals, but she wasn't at any of them. I waited and finally went to bed. Except that I just laid there and held the phone in my hands, and I periodically called her. Sometime during the night, I fell asleep, and my phone ringing woke me up. I thought it had to be Erin, and I was mad at her for making me worry. But it was the police. It was about six this morning. A delivery guy … found Erin's body in an alley. She didn't have her purse or ID on her, but the police checked and found that I'd called about her. They contacted me and asked if she was still missing. When I said yes, they described her." He paused and gulped. "I knew it was her. I had to go and identify the body. I talked to the police there, and then came home and the detectives came here for more questions."

I quickly wiped away a tear that had rolled down my cheek. "Caleb, I'm so sorry."

He nodded slowly. "I can't believe it." He drew in a breath and let it out heavily. "The detectives asked if I knew where Erin had been yesterday, and I didn't. I hadn't heard from her all day, but I only tried her when I got home, and not again until later in the evening." He gestured toward the window behind me. "Tiffany was over a while ago. She said that she'd seen Erin at the health club. She said Erin seemed fine, but she didn't know where Erin had gone after that. The detectives wanted to know if I'd seen Erin with any strangers, and I said I hadn't. They wanted to know if Erin had been acting weird, and she wasn't." He shrugged. "Everything was fine. We've been happy, and were even thinking about starting a family soon. I don't understand how this could happen." He wiped a hand over his face. "I don't know what I'm going to do without her." He choked up and cleared his throat.

"Um," I hesitated. "I can't believe I'm asking this, but Erin doesn't have any drug or mental issues?"

"Not at all." He didn't act offended that I'd asked.

"I thought you'd only talked to Tiffany last night," I said, thinking about what Kayla had told me.

He shook his head. "I called both of them."

I wondered why Melissa hadn't said she'd talked to Caleb, too.

"Is there anything I can help with?" I asked.

He shook his head. "Tiffany's already offered to bring some food over. Not that I've thought of eating. I called Erin's sister and she's going to call their mother."

"Where do they live?"

"Boston. They'll be coming out here soon to help with funeral arrangements." His lips formed a tight line. "I've never had to deal with something like this before. I don't even know where to begin with all that."

"There's time," I murmured.

He didn't say anything.

"Is it just Erin's sister and mother?"

"Yes," he said. "Her father died of a heart attack a few years ago."

I realized I didn't know anything about her family or his.

"Do you have relatives that can help?" I asked.

"I have a younger brother, but I'm not that close to him. My parents divorced, and I haven't even called my mother yet. She wasn't too keen on Erin, but I'm sure she'll come out for the funeral. I don't talk to my father much, either."

"If there's anything I can do to help, don't hesitate to ask."

"I appreciate that."

A long silence stretched between us, and he suddenly blinked hard.

"How are you doing?" he asked. "With everything with Rick?"

"I'll get through it," I said, touched that he'd thought to ask.

He and Rick weren't buddies, but they had golfed together some. I didn't know whether he cared that Rick wasn't around anymore.

"I hope you don't take this the wrong way," he said, "but I never thought Rick was right for you."

"It's okay."

I felt that thrill again. Was he presenting an opening for me? That stab of guilt slashed through me. I stood up before I did anything stupid.

"I should let you go."

He got up as well. "I've got phone calls to make."

He walked me to the door, and I reached out and touched his arm.

"Seriously, call me if you need anything."

He smiled. "I will."

I stepped onto the porch and he quietly shut the door. I went down the sidewalk and was about to cross the street when Tiffany's silver Mercedes backed out of her driveway. I stopped to let the car pass, and she rolled down the window. She leaned over so she could see my face.

"Don't act like you care," she snapped.

"Excuse me?"

"What did you do to her?"

"Who?" I glanced back at the McCormick house. "Erin?"

"We know you didn't like her," Tiffany said. "But to do this? Stay away from Caleb, you hear?"

The window rolled up and the Mercedes backed into the street and sped off. I stared at her car, stunned.

What was that all about? I slowly walked back to my house. I knew the neighbor women didn't like me, but why would they think I'd done something to Erin? I looked back at the McCormick house one last time and shook my head.

CHAPTER SIX

I went inside and stood looking into the back yard. It needed tending to, but I ignored that and fixed a salad for lunch. It was tasteless, and I didn't finish it. Then I sat for a long time with the TV on, but I wasn't really listening. I kept thinking about Caleb and Erin. Who would do that to her? It didn't make sense. Then my mind went to what Tiffany had said. It didn't take a genius to know the "we" she referred to – her and Melissa. Did they really think I could murder Erin? Talk about crazy. But then, things had happened between Erin and me. Maybe Melissa and Tiffany thought I disliked Erin so much, I'd kill her.

I finally got up, went into my office, and turned on the computer. I logged onto the Internet and searched Erin's name again. This time I found her Facebook page. She'd not put any limits on her privacy settings, and I was able to see everything about her, including her posts and who she was friends with.

She'd listed her hometown as Boston, and she'd gone to Smith College in Northampton, Massachusetts. She'd listed her work as a project coordinator.

"Somewhere in a past life," I muttered. I'd never known Erin to work at all.

I scrolled down the page and studied her friends. Melissa, Tiffany and a few other neighbors were there. Of course Erin hadn't wanted to friend me, not that I would ask. I knew she wouldn't respond.

I studied the pictures she'd posted. A lot were of her with Melissa and Tiffany, golfing and drinking at what I assumed was the clubhouse, as they had golf attire on. She looked happy.

One post was from a woman I didn't recognize, and Erin had been tagged in the photo. Her name was Laura Thackery. She was in a cute red dress, and she was pointing at her stomach, which protruded just slightly. I read the text associated with the picture.

"Look at my baby bump."

I stared at her face more closely. She was glowing. I felt a twinge of jealousy, wishing that had been something I could've posted about myself. I read through the comments, and noticed one from this woman to Erin.

"Is this going to be you someday?" Laura had written.

"Not anytime soon," Erin had replied.

What Caleb had said just hours ago rang in my ears. They'd been planning to start a family soon. Had he known what Erin was feeling about having children? Or had she been lying to her friend? I sighed, knowing that whatever Erin had thought had gone to her grave. I went back to Erin's list of friends and searched through it, but Caleb was not there. So whatever she'd posted on Facebook was safe from him, unless he specifically hunted through her page.

I scrolled through more pictures, many of Erin on expensive trips or at upscale restaurants. Some were of Erin with her mother and sister. Her sister – Anita – was a younger, and maybe slightly prettier, version of Erin. Both had dark blue eyes, long blond hair, and the same thin smiles. I could see a resemblance to their mother, although in this picture, Erin's mother had a frown on her face. In another, posted six months ago, a man was standing near the three of them, and I wondered who he was. I doubted it was Erin's father because Caleb had said he'd died a few years ago.

It was interesting seeing these snapshots of Erin's life, and I wondered who had murdered her. Was he somewhere in these pages? I certainly didn't know. There weren't any clues that I could see. Erin appeared to have lived a happy, if ostensibly wealthy, lifestyle. I had friends who weren't afraid to share their true feelings on Facebook, but Erin didn't appear to do that. If she'd been irritated or mad about anything, she hadn't hinted about that in her posts.

Here and there were pictures of her and Caleb. As I'd always thought, they appeared blissful. She looked relaxed, and Caleb was always smiling. I sat back and thought about the two of them. From an outsider's perspective, nothing had seemed wrong.

I went to my home page and looked through what I'd posted. It had been a while, and I saw some posts that were much whinier than I'd realized when I'd written them. In a few, my mother had chided me to be glad for the life I had. I shook my head. There were so many things that she didn't know or care about.

Farther down my page were posts with pictures of Rick. I gritted my teeth as I looked at them. At the time, I'd thought they were happy pictures, but as I stared at them now, I realized that wasn't the case. In most, Rick had a beer or some other alcoholic drink in his hand. In a lot of the pictures, he had a wild look in his eyes. That's who he was, even though I'd been ignorant of that side of him. I moved the mouse over to the caret in the corner of a post and deleted it. Then I did this with several more with Rick in them, thinking "Kristen would be proud of me."

I finally left Facebook and checked a few pages of search results for Erin McCormick, but I didn't find any more social media profiles, or anything else about her. I checked the *Denver Post* again to see if there were any articles about a body being found near the motel on Colfax, and it was the same result with the local news channel websites. Her death was either not going to make the news, or it was still too early. I kept searching until the phone interrupted me. I stared at the screen. It was Kristen.

"You need to sign the papers," she said without any greeting. "It's been over a week. Plenty of time."

"All right."

I waited for her reply, and it was a long time coming.

"Are you okay?" she asked. "You sound funny. Are you going to fight me on this?"

She knew me well enough to detect something in just two words.

"No," I said. "Erin's dead."

"Who? Oh, the woman down the street? Caleb's wife?" She was surprised.

"Yes."

"What happened?"

I related everything I'd learned from the police and Caleb, and what Tiffany had said to me. And I told her where Erin's body had been found.

"You don't think she was at that motel with Rick?" was the first thing she asked when I was finished. There was acid in her tone. "He wasn't ever with her, was he?"

"Of course not."

"Well, Rick did get around."

"It's not as bad as you've made it out to be," I snapped.

"Uh-huh." She let out a long, patient breath. "Look, honey, I'm sorry. I shouldn't have said that."

"It's okay."

She made a clicking sound with her tongue. "You've got a lot going on, and you need to take care of yourself. You have things you need to do, so focus on that right now, okay? Don't worry about Caleb. He's got people around to help him out. I need you to work with me and take care of Rick, so you can move on. He's got his lawyer pressuring me, and we've got to get this moving along."

"I'll take care of it." I glanced out the window, toward the McCormick house. "I told Caleb if he needed anything, he should call. But I'll read the paperwork and let you know what I think," I tacked on quickly. "I promise."

"I'm giving you twenty-four hours. Then I'm coming over and we're going to discuss things."

"Okay," I said, sounding petulant.

I was slightly irritated with her pushiness, and yet I knew I needed that, and a bigger part of me was grateful for her. She laughed and ended the call. I'd no sooner set down the phone before it rang again. I recognized the number and dread passed over me.

"Hello, Rick," I said.

"I haven't heard from you. Why haven't you responded?"

"I've been busy."

Two could be just as irritated as one.

"Dammit, Amber. Get off your ass and sign the papers I left you."

My pulse quickened, but I didn't say anything.

"I want to move on, and I can't until I get our divorce finalized."

"You want to, or you already have?"

It was quiet on the other end of the line.

"Is there someone else?" I continued.

"Of course not."

I didn't believe him. There was already another woman. There'd probably been several.

"What's the matter?" he finally asked.

"Did you hear about Erin?"

"What about her?"

"She's dead."

The sound of him drawing in a breath was loud. "What happened?"

I told him, just like I'd told Kristen. He was silent when I finished.

"You liked her, didn't you?" I asked.

"Sure I did. That was no secret. But not as much as you liked Caleb."

He'd made me feel guilty about Caleb before, and I felt guilty now. Then I thought about what Kristen had said, and this time, I didn't let him deflect the conversation from himself.

"Did you sleep with her?"

"What? No."

He said it too quickly, his tone too casual, and I wondered if he was lying. I'd only confronted him about Erin once, after I'd seen him with her on the street last summer. He'd just come home from work, and she had been out walking. They'd been intimate as they talked, both smiling. Then she'd reached out and put a hand on his arm. The smile stayed plastered on her face, and she flicked her hair as she talked and laughed. There was something in the whole exchange that hadn't seemed right. When he'd come in the house, I'd asked him if there was something going on with Erin. He'd denied it, and quickly brought up my behavior with Caleb. I'd believed him then, but I didn't now.

"You jerk," I said. My stomach roiled.

"I did not sleep with Erin." His words were slow and deliberate. "I'll admit there were other women, but she wasn't one of them. And who do you think you are, accusing me of having an affair with Erin when you slept with Caleb."

"I did not!" I said forcefully.

It was true, and he knew it.

"When's the last time you saw Erin?" I asked.

"What? I don't know. Months ago."

"You talked to her the last time you were here. A week ago. The day she died. Did you set up a time to meet her at that motel, and then kill her?"

"I always knew you were crazy, and this confirms it," he said.

"When's the last time you were at the Standard Motel?"

"I don't know. A long time ago."

I didn't believe him. "Did you see her there?"

"Amber, I don't know what you're talking about, but leave it alone. It's in the past. Just sign the paperwork and be done with it." He swore and ended the call.

I took the phone away from my ear and slowly set it down. I stared at my laptop for a long time, then looked at the clock. It was after four. I went back to Facebook and found a picture of Erin that was a close-up of her face, then copied and printed it. I took it and my phone, went into the kitchen for my purse and car keys, and left the house.

CHAPTER SEVEN

The Standard Motel was a dive on Colfax east of Sheridan Street. As I drove there, my mind wandered to the first time I'd actually been there. I'd driven past it numerous times, never giving much thought to the place. But I became really aware of it after I found out Rick had been going there.

He and I had been married for almost a year, and his job was going well. We'd just moved into the new house, and I was about to quit my job, even though I kind of liked it. The idea of a new place to live, with enough room for a family, had been everything I thought I wanted.

Rick had been extremely busy with his work, and he'd been stressed. His drinking had grown more intense than usual, and so had some of our fights. Our relationship had always been somewhat volatile, but our making up had been just as passionate. That whole thing of hard fights and great make-up sex fit us perfectly. He had been coming home late, always saying it was because he had to stay late at work. Even now, as I drove on Colfax, I thought about how stupid I'd been. I should've seen the signs. He'd come home with alcohol on his breath. That wasn't anything unusual, but the occasional perfume scent that lingered about him – which wasn't mine – was. I'd turned a blind eye to it.

Then one evening when he came home from work, he'd gone

upstairs to change, saying he had to go to a meeting at the Sheraton downtown. His phone was on the counter, and it lit up with a text. Before the screen went black, I saw the first part of the text.

"The Standard, right? I'll be late."

When he came back downstairs, I asked again where he was going. He said he had a meeting downtown, something he couldn't get out of. He'd acted like it was a pain, that he'd rather be home with me. Then he kissed me on the lips and headed out the door. I waited a while, telling myself that it wasn't anything, that I must've read the text wrong. I'd finally looked up the address for the motel, grabbed my keys, and left.

When I got there, I parked down the street and looked into the parking lot. I'd just been thinking I was crazy, that he wasn't anywhere around, when I saw a dark blue Lexus. I got out of my car, sneaked into the parking lot, and up to the car. I glanced around, making sure no one was watching me, then peeked into the window. It was Rick's. Easy to tell because he had my wedding garter hanging from the rearview mirror, and his sunglasses were where he'd put them around the gear shift.

I went back to my Beemer and sat behind the wheel, waiting and crying, because I knew. I tried to tell myself that Rick was at this sleazy motel for the business meeting he'd said, but even I wasn't that dumb. The motel was the kind of place you went to for sex and not much else.

So many things ran through my mind. Was he carrying on an affair, or was he seeing prostitutes? Should I get checked for STDs? I swore at Rick. I thought about going to talk to whoever was at the check-in desk to see if I could get his room number, and to find out how often he'd been there, but the thought terrified me, both because I wasn't the type to confront a stranger like that, and because I really didn't want to know the answer.

I finally wiped away my tears and drove home. Rick had told me he'd be late, so I poured a glass of wine and took a long bath, crying the whole time. I went to bed, but just laid there in the dark. It was very late when I heard the garage door open. I rolled over on my side, my back to the bedroom door.

Rick came quietly into the room, but kept the light off. He tiptoed into the bathroom and an outline of light appeared around the closed door. I heard water running, then the light went out. He emerged and slipped under the cover. I didn't turn to him. He breathed quietly.

"Who is she?" I finally asked.

His body went rigid. "What?"

"Don't lie to me."

He didn't say anything.

"I want you to stop seeing her," I said.

He ground his teeth, then let out a long sigh. "Okay."

We never spoke about it again. I think he did go back to the motel, at least a few more times, but I never confronted him about it. He was different for a while, more loving and attentive. We bought the house and moved, and things appeared to be good.

I'd shared with Kristen about the affair. She had been supportive of me, but she also told me that she wasn't surprised by what he'd done. That hurt as much as anything, that she had been more in tune with Rick's true nature than I had been. I knew she'd not been overly fond of him, but her true feelings became more evident over time. She'd encouraged me to divorce him then, but I'd told her things were working themselves out, and that Rick and I would make it through. And it seemed like we had. Or that's what I'd told myself. Kristen kept her mouth shut after that, but as I looked back on it, I knew she'd figured things were headed in the direction where they were now.

By now I'd pulled into the Standard Motel parking lot. I got out and went into the small front office. A little old man sat behind a short counter. He was watching a game show on TV and he glanced over at me, bored, but then his eyes widened in surprise. Even though I wasn't dressed in anything fancy, I suspected I was a cut above his usual clientele.

"Do you need a room, miss?" he asked cautiously.

"No, thank you." I walked up to the counter. "I'm wondering if you could tell me whether a certain man has been here." I reached into my purse. "I have his picture."

He hesitated, as if he'd been asked this before, and he didn't want to answer. He settled on evasive. "We get guys coming around."

"It's really important to me." I had my wallet out, and I flipped to a picture of Rick.

He put his hands on the counter and stared at me. I showed him the picture.

"Has he been around here lately?"

He pursed his lips and studied the photo. "I don't think so."

"How often do you work?"

"I'm here most nights from three until midnight."

I nodded. "This man came here for a while a couple of years ago. I know that's been a while, but –"

"I've worked here a long time, but I couldn't tell you that far back. Got lots of people coming and going."

I laughed, even though I couldn't put any humor behind it.

"You're sure you haven't seen him around lately?" I asked. "What about a week ago, on Sunday night?"

"When that woman was found in the alley?"

"That's right."

"Hmm. That was a busy night. I don't remember him here."

"What about the woman?" I pulled out the picture of Erin that I'd printed and showed it to him. "Has she ever been around here?"

He barely looked at the picture. "The police showed me a picture of her."

"The police were here?"

He nodded.

"Was she here that night?" I repeated.

He shook his head. "Not that I recall. I don't know if I've ever seen her around. Tends to be the guys that come in and pay for the rooms, you know? Couples don't come in together."

"Oh, right." I studied him. "Would you tell me or the police if you had seen her, or this man?" I pointed at the wallet picture.

He shrugged. "I don't want to deal with the police."

"Why is that?"

He waved a hand around. "Lady, if word got around that I talked to the police, my business would go in the toilet, you know what I'm saying?"

"I see," I murmured.

"I keep my mouth shut, that's how it goes."

Something occurred to me. I picked up my wallet and pulled out a twenty. "You're *sure* you haven't seen this man around here?"

He stared at the money and then gave the photo another good look.

"I'm divorcing him," I explained. "This will help me with all the legal stuff. I need to know if he's been lying to me."

He rubbed his jaw. "He's been in, but I couldn't tell you when. A while ago."

"How long?"

He shrugged. "I don't know. A few weeks? Maybe other times."

"But not with this woman."

"No. I don't remember seeing her around."

"Thanks." I handed him the money, then stuffed Erin's picture back in my purse. "Did you ever see the woman my husband was with?"

He shook his head again. "But I did see your guy go across the street to the Starbucks. Maybe they know something."

I thanked him again and walked outside. I couldn't walk to my car fast enough to get away from all that the motel represented. I fought traffic and arrived home near five-thirty. I parked and then walked down the drive to the mailbox. John Caruthers was just getting his mail.

"You heard about Erin?" I called out.

He whirled around, his face tense. "Oh ... yeah. Tiffany called me at work. She was pretty upset."

"I can't believe it happened."

He nodded. "What do the police know?"

"I haven't heard much."

I decided not to tell him about my suspicions, or about how Tiffany was treating me.

We both looked toward the McCormick house.

"Did you know Erin very well?" I asked.

He ran a hand through his hair. "We all hung out some. But I wouldn't say I really knew her. She and Tiffany were friends." He glanced back at his house. "Tiffany will wonder where I am."

"Sure," I said. "Have a good night."

"You, too."

He turned and hurried up the drive and into his garage. I looked at Caleb's house, then walked slowly up the walk and through my front door, symbolically shutting out the questions surrounding Erin's death.

If only it were that easy.

CHAPTER EIGHT

I tossed and turned that night, my dreams a mix of Caleb, Erin, and Rick. At times the dreams had Erin and Rick together, living in the McCormick house. They had a great life. She was still the country club queen, but Rick was sober and settled. I was with Caleb, and yet, in the weird way dreams were, it wasn't really him, but more of an amalgam of him and my father. And I was myself, and yet also my mother. And it wasn't the ideal marriage that I'd picture with Caleb, but of my mother's lifeless, loveless marriage for which she'd settled. I wasn't happy at all.

I awoke before dawn and lay for a long time. Slivers of hazy light crept around the window blinds. I put on my robe and plodded downstairs to make coffee. I turned the TV to the early news, but didn't hear anything about Erin, so I brought my laptop into the den and while the TV anchors droned on, I checked the online news websites. On one I found the mention of a woman's body being found in an alley near the Standard Motel. Her name was being withheld, and the details of her death were scant. I'd gotten more from Caleb and the police. The police suspected foul play, and they didn't have any people of interest at this time.

So who had killed her?

As the *Today* show started, I got up, took my coffee and went to the living room window, expecting Caleb to drive by at his usual time. Then I realized that with everything that had happened, he was likely not going into work anytime soon.

I stood in the window for a long time, as I'd done for too many days to count. My coffee grew cold. Melissa Lowenstein's car backed out of the driveway. I couldn't tell whether or not she wore her golf attire. Then a sedan came down the street and pulled into Caleb's driveway. Detectives Maddow and Kowalski got out and strode purposefully up to the front porch.

Why were they back? I thought. Had they found Erin's killer?

Neither looked around as Maddow pressed the doorbell with her finger. A moment later Caleb opened the door. I strained to see his face but couldn't. They stepped inside and the door shut. I stared at the McCormick house for a long time. I should've been doing something else, like working in the yard or going to the health club, but I couldn't pull myself away from the window.

Half an hour passed and the detectives were still with Caleb. I finally went to the kitchen and dumped out my cold coffee, then went upstairs, took a quick shower and got dressed. When I peeked out my bedroom window, the sedan was still there. Whatever the detectives were discussing with Caleb was taking a long time. I hoped it was that they'd found Erin's killer so that Caleb could have some closure and move on. I turned away from the window as my mind said, "Move on to me."

I went back to the living room. The TV droned on in the other room, and the minutes ticked by. I kept telling myself I needed to look at the paperwork Kristen and Rick had left, but I didn't feel like it right now. It could wait.

Another hour passed and the detectives finally came out of the

McCormick house. They strolled to their car and backed out into the street. I stepped back as the car passed slowly by. I couldn't be sure, but I thought Detective Maddow looked at my window. When the car was gone, I moved back to where I could see the street. I waited to see if Tiffany or any other neighbor would emerge, but no one did. I slipped outside, hurried across the street, and up to Caleb's door. I rang the bell and waited. He took a long time to answer.

"Hey, Amber" he said when he saw me. He forced a smile.

He looked tired, his eyes red-rimmed. He hadn't shaved, and his shirt was wrinkled. Not the neat and tidy Caleb I was used to. I realized I didn't know what to say. It was mostly my curiosity that had brought me here.

"I ... saw the detectives were here," I said.

"Oh?" he said, as if my knowing that was a surprise.

He didn't fool me. Of course he'd know because I was at the window. I was *always* at the window.

"Do they know who murdered Erin?"

"No." He stepped back. "Why don't you come in?"

"Sure."

As I passed by him, I got a whiff of soap, and not his usual co-logne. We went into the living room and sat down. He opened his mouth wide and drew in a deep breath, then let it out loudly.

"They're focusing on me, wanting to know what I did the day Erin died."

"They think you may have killed her." I'd been wondering when we'd get to that.

He nodded slowly. "I'm not surprised. They always look at the spouse because the spouse is frequently involved. It doesn't make it any easier answering their questions."

"What did they ask you?"

He looked away. "I don't know how much I should say."

"I understand. I'm just trying to help."

He swiped a hand across his forehead. "I know." He seemed to soften some. "I guess it can't hurt to tell you. They wanted me to account for my whereabouts the entire day Erin was killed."

"You were at work, right?"

"Yes, but I did go to lunch that day by myself."

"Where at?"

"Smash Burger, on the mall. There were lots of people there, but I doubt anyone would remember me specifically."

"Is that when they think Erin was killed?"

"No. That time probably isn't concerning them." He grimaced. "Or maybe it is. Who knows? Everyone at work can account for me in the morning and afternoon, but when I left work, I came straight home. I was here the entire evening. I'm sure they'll check with all of you to see if anyone saw me leave that night. Of course they won't find anyone who saw me leave, because I didn't."

I thought back to what I'd done that evening. I'm sure I'd looked out the window for a while because I did that a lot. I'd seen Caleb come home from work, but he hadn't seen me in the window that evening. I hadn't seen Erin all day, and I didn't see either one of them that night. But I wasn't at the window the whole evening. I'd lain in bed that night for the longest time, and … it suddenly dawned on me.

"I heard your car that night," I said. "I saw headlights and then you drove past."

He shook his head. "That wasn't me. I didn't go out."

He acted so sure, I thought I must've been mistaken.

"You said you'd talked to Tiffany and Melissa that night," I said.

"I talked to them on the phone. The police can find the records of that from the phone companies, but I could've been somewhere else when I called them."

"The police pointed that out?"

He nodded.

"What about your computer or your laptop?" I suggested. "Were you on either of those in the evening?"

He shrugged. "No, and that wouldn't prove anything."

"It might if you were on the Internet. They might be able to pinpoint your location when you were on the computer."

"That's a good thought, but I was here, and not on the computer."

"What about your phone? Do you have a landline?"

"Not for a long time."

"There must be a way for the phone company to tell that when you made those phone calls, they connected through a tower around here."

"I would think so, but I only called Erin once when I got home, and not again until it got late. As the detectives pointed out, I could've gone out for at least a few hours, then come back here and called her cell phone later in the evening. There was plenty of time for me to ..." He hesitated, "kill her and then come home."

I didn't want to say anything, but he was right. It looked bad for him.

"Do the police know when she was killed?" I asked.

"Sometime that evening. They're not sharing with me exactly when. She could've been in that alley all evening long. Certainly plenty of time for me to be there for a while."

"Do they have any witnesses? Anyone who saw something?"

"If they do, they're not saying."

"But you weren't at the motel, right?"

He stared at me, and I wasn't sure if I'd offended him.

"I was here all evening," he finally said. He frowned. "They're looking into my finances, trying to find a motive. Did I have an insurance policy on Erin, that kind of thing."

"Did you?" I murmured.

"Yes. A million dollars on each of us."

That shouldn't have surprised me, but it was still a lot of money.

"I don't need the money," he said. "I told them our finances are in order. We don't have a lot of debt, besides the house and cars, and I'm not involved in anything, like a shady deal at work, or something where I need money. I would have no reason to murder my wife."

"What did they say to that?"

"Sometimes people kill for the smallest reasons."

"And they're going to try to find that."

He shrugged. "They wanted to know how we were getting along…" His voice trailed off.

I remembered he'd said that everything between them was fine, but maybe – if that wasn't the case – he'd be more open to sharing now. "How *were* you two doing?" I finally asked.

He got up and began to pace, a few steps toward a large fireplace, then back toward the couch.

"Things were good. I've been a little busy at work, but I don't think it bothered Erin that much. She was golfing and doing the usual things she does. There's nothing there for the police to think I killed her. They asked if I was having an affair and I laughed. That is so not me.

Then they asked if *she* was having an affair, and I said that wasn't the case, either, that she'd never do that to me. We were in love." He stopped and put his hands on his hips. "I know they have to ask all of that, but it's absurd. And it isn't easy to hear."

"I'm sure it's not," I said softly, then added, "You're sure?"

"There wasn't anything."

I thought about my suspicions about Rick and Erin, and a wave of relief passed over me. I was wrong about that. There might've been sparks between the two of them – as I felt with Caleb – but Rick hadn't acted on it. As I looked at Caleb, I felt sorry for him. Deep down, I knew he would never have done anything to hurt Erin, and to be accused of that had to hurt him deeply.

"Did they find out anything about Erin? Why was she in that area of town?"

"If they know anything about that, they didn't share it with me. They asked me that again, and I told them the same thing I'd said when they were first here. I don't know why Erin was in that area. I suppose it's possible she was killed somewhere else and dumped in that alley."

"Did you suggest that?"

He nodded. "I'm sure they've thought of that, but if that was the case, they're not saying."

He went back to pacing. "I started to look around the house, searching for any clue as to what she might've been doing, some explanation for why she was near that motel, but I can't find a thing."

"Nothing?" I felt bad asking it.

"No. Her phone was gone, and I don't know how to access her messages. The police said they'd see if they could get a warrant to get the records. I don't know if that'll happen, though. And I don't know what they'd find on it."

"What about her credit cards? Did you check your statements to see what purchases she made that day?"

"There wasn't anything, but Erin liked to use cash for things. Don't ask me why. I did check with our bank, and she'd withdrawn a few hundred dollars the day before she died. But that wasn't anything unusual." He stopped pacing again and leaned against the couch. "Erin's mother and sister are coming into town the day after tomorrow. I'm sure the police are going to talk to them some more."

"They already have?"

"Yes, but I'm sure the police will have more questions. Who knows, maybe her mother or sister can shed some light on all this. But when I talked to them, neither one said they knew of anything out of the ordinary."

He stared past me, out the window, and I watched him. Something was going on behind his eyes, but I couldn't tell what.

"The police will look into me, but they're not going to find anything because I didn't kill Erin. And they won't find anything with her, either."

"I know it's hard," I said. "But should you be asking around, maybe at the health club or the golf course?"

"Asking what?"

I hesitated. "To see what Erin might've been doing. Maybe some-one knows something you don't."

"The police will do that. And if I ask around, that might make me look suspicious."

I was a little surprised he wasn't more inquisitive, but he made a good point about the police. I was curious, though.

"Is there anything I can do to help?" I asked.

"I appreciate the offer, but there isn't anything right now. I'm still stunned by all this."

I stood up. "Make sure you're taking care of yourself. You need to eat. Would you like to come over for lunch? I can fix you a sandwich or something."

He shook his head. "That's very nice of you, but I'm doing okay. Really, I am."

I nodded, and he walked me to the door. As I stepped outside, he put a hand on my shoulder.

"I do appreciate your concern," he said. "I know Erin could be a little distant sometimes, but she did like you."

I wasn't sure why he said that, because it clearly hadn't been the case. Or had I missed something? He thanked me again, and I said I'd be in touch. He threw me a wan smile and the door closed.

As I walked back across the street, I noticed that the police sedan was parked in front of Melissa's house. Detectives Maddow and Kowalski were waiting on her porch. Maddow rang the bell as I dashed across the street, wondering what they would think if they saw me coming from the McCormick house. As I reached my porch, I glanced over my shoulder. The detectives were stepping away from Melissa's house. She must not have been home. I rushed inside and quietly shut the door. I leaned against it, hoping they would go to Tiffany's house next. Seconds ticked by.

Then the doorbell rang.

CHAPTER NINE

"Detective Maddow," I said when I opened the door. "What can I do for you?"

I didn't address Kowalski because he'd remained silent the last time I'd seen them. Maddow stood with her hands on her hips, with Kowalski just behind her.

"We'd like to ask you a few more questions," she said, "if you have a few minutes."

I thought about all the TV shows and movies I'd seen, where the person of interest always asks to speak to a lawyer before they talk to the police. But what did I have to hide? And I'd feel foolish calling and bothering Kristen. I figured I could handle this myself, so I stepped back and let them in. They went right into the living room. Maddow sat where she had before, and Kowalski leaned in the doorway as he'd done when they were first here. He took off his dark sunglasses and crossed his arms.

"I noticed you talked to Caleb earlier today," I said, attempting to take control of the conversation.

Maddow stared at me. "We're in the middle of a murder investigation."

I put my hands in my lap and nodded.

"What were you doing the night she was killed? Sunday night?" she went on. "You were here at home that evening?"

Her assumption was correct. I hadn't been out in a long time.

"That's right," I said.

"And you did what?"

I shrugged. "I watched TV." It sounded lame, as if I had a boring life, which I did.

"All evening?"

"I think so."

She narrowed her eyes. "You think so, or you know so?"

"It was all evening," I said sheepishly.

She glanced into the hall. "No one was here with you?"

"Of course not."

Was she thinking that Caleb had been here that night?

"What TV shows did you watch?"

I honestly couldn't remember what I watched each evening. The shows were just noise in the background that blended together while my mind wandered. "*NCIS: New Orleans*, I think." I watched the show some, but couldn't remember the last time I'd seen an episode.

She made a show of pulling a small notepad and pen from her coat pocket. She wrote down something, then looked back at me. Kowalski stared at me without a word.

"Is there a problem?" I asked. For the first time, I wondered if I should call Kristen. But my legs felt like lead and I stayed in my seat.

"We're just trying to figure things out," Maddow said. "Caleb said he was home for the entire evening. Did you see him that night?"

She'd asked me that before.

"Just when he came home from work," I said. "Not after that."

"You like to watch out the window?"

I hesitated. "Sometimes, I guess. But I don't remember that night specifically."

"You're in the middle of a divorce."

"That's right."

"Your husband, Rick. Has he been around here lately?"

"He showed up the day that Erin was killed, to give me some papers to sign."

"Did he see Erin that day?"

"They talked on the street for a moment, before Rick drove off."

"Were they friendly?"

"I guess so." For some reason, I held back how Erin had appeared to get upset with Rick, right before he sped away. "You think Rick had something to do with her death?"

"Why would you ask that?"

All my thoughts about Rick and his past behavior raced through my head. He was a heel, but I couldn't believe he would hurt anyone.

"No reason," I finally said.

"Do you know what Rick was doing that night?"

"He hasn't lived here in six months."

"Does that mean you don't know?"

"Yes, I don't know. I don't talk to Rick."

"Except when he drops by."

I stared at her. "Yes."

"Did he have any routines when you were married? Anything that he might've done on Sunday nights?"

"He liked to go to Benjamin's Bar on the way home from work, and sometimes on weekends, but I have no idea if he was there that night."

She nodded, her face blank. I couldn't tell whether I'd given her something she already knew. And did it matter?

"Tell me about your relationship with the McCormicks," Maddow said.

"We've been over this."

"Tell me again."

I sighed. "We didn't do much with them." I let the statement hang in the air.

"What about *you*?" she asked pointedly.

"I didn't know them very well."

"You met them when you moved in?" she prompted.

"Yes."

"How often did you socialize with them?"

"We had a barbecue or two, but that's all."

Maddow's eyes narrowed again. "Your neighbors have indicated that they golf with Erin and workout at the health club with her, and have drinks regularly. You don't do that with them?"

I shook my head. "No, I'm not part of their group."

"Why not?"

"I don't know. I was never asked to be a part of their ..." I started to say clique, but left it off.

"Hmm," she said.

"What does that mean?" I retorted.

Kowalski shifted on his feet, but remained silent. The last time they were here, I'd been able to ignore him. This time I felt as if he were seeing through me, to all my secrets. I surreptitiously wiped my sweaty hands on my jeans.

"I heard you did go to the health club with Erin and," she gestured at the window, "some of the other neighbors."

"Well, yes, but I haven't been to the health club in a long while. And I didn't go with them."

She pursed her lips at that. "Some of the women in the neighborhood said Erin wasn't fond of you."

I tried for indifferent. "Oh?"

"They had a clear impression that you were strongly attracted to her husband."

"Caleb?" I said innocently. I glanced away. "I don't think so. He seems to be a nice man, but I hardly spoke to him." The last part was true, the rest wasn't. Could she tell I was lying?

"Just because you didn't speak to him doesn't mean you didn't want something to happen with him."

"Are you asking if I had an affair with Caleb?" I snapped.

She arched an eyebrow.

I took a calming breath. "Did you ask Caleb that?"

She nodded.

Wow, I thought. He hadn't shared that with me. "To answer your question, I did not have an affair with Caleb."

"I talked with Tiffany this morning," she said. "She thinks something was up with you and Mr. McCormick almost from the first day you met him."

I'd wondered if Melissa and Tiffany had said something to the police about Caleb and me. I knew they were upset about Erin, and I figured they were looking to lash out at any target. But after a day had passed, and they'd had a chance to think things through … to still think that about me a day later. That hurt.

She changed the subject. "How often did you argue with Erin?"

"Excuse me? I never had an argument with Erin."

I was getting more agitated, my voice rising.

"I heard that you and Erin had some harsh words for each other."

I remembered a time after we'd had the barbecue. I'd been walking down the street and Caleb was washing his car. I'd hardly said hello to him when Erin flew out of the house and said that Caleb needed to come in to take a phone call. Once he'd gone inside, she turned on me with venom in her voice, telling me to leave Caleb alone. I'd been taken aback by her aggressive tone.

"What do you mean?" I'd asked.

"Don't play dumb," she'd replied. "I know you have problems with Rick, but don't drag us into anything."

Maddow cleared her throat. "Ms. Aldridge?"

I dismissed the memory. "I guess we weren't the best of friends," I said. "But I didn't wish her any harm."

"You had a fight with her a few weeks ago."

"No," I said quickly. I fought to think of any argument I'd had with Erin, but came up empty. There hadn't been anything. "I hadn't talked to her in weeks."

She glanced at her notes. "You had a fight with Erin, and she said, 'Stay away from my husband or else.' And you said she should back off or else. I heard that you were quite angry. And threatening."

"That's not true," I said.

Her expression stayed neutral, but her eyes flickered. She thought I was lying.

"So no fights with Erin?" she said.

"No," I said softly.

She tapped her fingertips together and moved on. "Did you see anything unusual the night Erin was murdered?"

"Detective Maddow, I've already been over this–" I suddenly stopped.

"Yes?"

"There was a car."

"What car?"

I thought back. "There's been a dark car around at night. I saw it about a week before Erin was killed. I saw it a time or two."

"Where was it parked?"

I got up and pointed down the street to where I'd seen it. "It was a few houses down from the McCormick's."

She leaned forward in her seat and looked out the window. "What's the make and model?"

"I don't know."

I held back that I wondered if it could've been Rick's car.

"You saw the car before Erin was killed?"

"Yes."

"How long did it sit there?"

"I don't know. I watched the street for a while and then went to bed."

"Was anyone in the car?"

"I couldn't tell."

"And you didn't get a license plate number." The slight derisive note was clear.

"It was too dark to tell." Did she think I spied on the neighborhood with binoculars?

"Have you seen the car since Erin was murdered?"

"No."

"You don't have any idea who the car might belong to?"

I shook my head. "No idea."

"Was it there the night Erin was killed?"

"Not when I looked, but I didn't watch the street the whole evening," I said defensively.

"How long *did* you look out the window?"

"I don't keep track of that."

Her eyes were suspicious slits, but I remained silent. She glanced at Kowalski, but his face didn't change expression.

"Don't you think that's significant?" I asked. "Maybe someone was stalking Erin."

"I'll make a note of it," Maddow said, although she didn't write anything down. "Why didn't you tell us this before?"

"I forgot."

"I see. Is there anything else strange in the last few weeks that you've noticed?"

"No, just the car."

"Did Mr. and Mrs. McCormick ever argue?"

"Not that I saw. They had a good relationship."

"Are you sure you're not saying that because you like Mr. McCormick?"

"Not at all," I said weakly. "Have you found out something about Erin?"

She didn't reply to that. "Do you own any tools?"

"Like a hammer or saw?" It suddenly dawned on me what she was asking. "You said she was killed with a blunt object. You think it was a hammer?"

She stared at me. "Do you play softball or baseball?"

"You think I did that to Erin?" I was incredulous.

She didn't say a word.

"You've got to be kidding," I said. "You think because the neighbor women said Erin and I got into a fight that I'd kill her?"

"You seemed to want what Erin had. The house, the good husband. The neighbors say you've said you'd kill for a life like that."

"That's absurd."

"We have to look at everything."

"You're nuts. I think our discussion is over," I said. "If you want to talk to me further, you can do it with my lawyer present."

It sounded so official, and so late. Somewhere in my exchange with Maddow it should've occurred to me to stop and call Kristen, but I'd been caught up in my emotions. I hoped I wouldn't regret that decision.

Maddow nodded, stood up, and put her notepad and pen back in her pocket. I escorted them to the door.

"Thank you for your time," Maddow said as they stepped outside.

I shut the door and peered through the peephole. They stood on the porch for a long time, waiting. I'm sure they were trying to intimidate me, and it was working. My knees shook. They finally walked down the sidewalk and crossed the street, then went to Melissa Lowenstein's house. She must have come home while the detectives were with me, because after they rang the bell, she answered. The detectives disappeared inside, and I gulped. Who knew what Melissa would say about me?

I gazed through the peephole for another minute, then my legs gave out and I sank to the floor. I leaned against the door and cried.

CHAPTER TEN

I don't know how long I sat curled up against the door. I kept thinking how anyone could imagine that I murdered Erin. I would never have wanted to see Caleb in anguish like he was. In my befuddled state, I didn't realize how much I was focusing on him, rather than her.

The tile floor suddenly felt cold and hard. I wiped the tears from my cheeks and hauled myself to my feet. I peeked through the peephole again. The detectives' sedan was gone. I trudged into the kitchen and splashed cold water on my face. My hands shook. I grabbed the edge of the counter and stared blankly out the back window. The sun filtered through the trees, the rays a soft yellow on the lawn.

I found my cell phone and called Kristen. She was in a meeting, and I instructed the woman who answered to have Kristen call me as soon as she got out. The woman asked if I wanted her to interrupt the meeting. I couldn't bring myself to do that. I'd already done the damage in talking to the detectives, I could wait to tell Kristen about my foolishness.

After the call, I stood and stared out the back window again, my mind hazy. After a while, I became aware of noises in the other yard. Kayla was in her back yard with Talon. I went outside and crossed to the edge of the deck, where I could see over the fence. I called to Kayla. She turned, saw me, and hesitated.

"Oh, Amber, hello," she said. "How're you doing?" The cheeriness in her voice seemed forced.

"I'm all right." I glanced toward the street, then back to her. "Hey, have the police talked to you again? About Erin?"

She nodded. "They were over this morning." She crossed her arms, then looked at Talon, who was lying on a big blanket on the lawn.

"And?" I prompted.

She frowned. "They wanted to know if I'd noticed any strangers in the neighborhood, or if there'd been anything unusual that had happened recently."

"Did you ever see a dark-colored car around here at night? Maybe in the last few weeks? It might've been parked down the street from the McCormick house."

Her brow furrowed. "That doesn't sound familiar." Then she let out a nervous laugh. "The only dark car I know from around here is Rick's blue Lexus. Was it him?"

I shrugged and changed the subject. "Did the police ask you anything about me?"

"Well…"

"You won't hurt my feelings."

She blushed. "They did ask if I'd seen you fight with Erin."

I leaned into the railing. "What'd you tell them?"

"You remember that time before Thanksgiving? Right before …"

"Rick left," I finished.

"Right."

I could easily picture that time. Rick and I were constantly fighting, and he had been growing increasingly volatile. He'd never gotten physical with me, but I'd thought a time or two that he would be capable of that.

"You yelled at Erin," she went on.

Right then, all I could see was Rick, his face twisted in anger.

"Rick had come home from work," she said, "and he was out in the driveway talking to Erin. I heard you shout at him to come into the house."

"Oh, yeah," I said, trying to pretend that I couldn't remember it.

But I did, all too well. I'd been furious with Rick because he'd been out the night before, hadn't even bothered to come home, let alone call me to tell me where he was. I'd lain awake all night, wondering who he was with. When I'd gone outside and seen him with Erin, laughing and carrying on, I saw red. How could that jerk act like everything was fine after what he'd done to me?

Kayla cleared her throat. "You were so mad. I could hear it in your voice. And then you told Erin to go on home. You sounded so disdainful."

I couldn't find any words to say.

"I'm sorry, Amber, but I remembered that and I had to tell the detectives. I'm sure it's not a big deal."

"It's okay." I worked to recover my train of thought. "The detectives said I had a fight with Erin a few weeks ago, that she'd told me to stay away from her husband."

"I never heard her say that to you."

I breathed a sigh of relief. At least one of the neighbors knew the truth. My phone rang and I glanced at the screen. Kristen.

"I have to get this," I said.

"Sure. If you need anything, stop by." It was a halfhearted

invitation. "I know things must be hard, with Rick and all."

"I'll get through it."

She nodded and whirled around. She couldn't get to her daughter – and away from me – fast enough. I headed into the house as I answered the phone.

"What's going on?" Kristen asked. "Is there a problem with Rick?"

"No, it's worse. The police think I had something to do with Erin's death."

She swore. "You talked to them?"

"Yes. I know I shouldn't have, but I didn't think they suspected me of anything."

"Are they there now?"

"No, they left and talked to the other neighbors."

More curse words. "Stay there. I'm on my way over."

***

Forty-five minutes later, the doorbell rang. I'd barely unlocked the door when Kristen flew into the house. She stalked down the hall to the kitchen, her perfume a tornado in her wake. She was more than a little irritated with me.

"You talked to the police." She threw her purse down on the counter. "Without a lawyer present."

"Come on, Kristen. In the cop shows, they make it sound like you need a lawyer no matter what. But I didn't think there'd be any harm talking to them. How was I supposed to know they might be looking at me as a suspect?"

She let out a big sigh. "I wish you would've called me."

"I know," I said, duly chastised. "I didn't think it would matter. It wasn't until we were into the conversation that I realized they thought I might be involved in Erin's death."

She pulled out a kitchen chair and sat down. "Tell me everything."

I did. When I finished, she was shaking her head.

"It's all circumstantial," she said, her fingernail tapping the table. "But the fact that they're asking is not good."

"I can't believe they think I'd do anything to hurt Caleb."

Her eyebrows rose. "You're more worried about him than her," she said.

I tipped my head and shrugged. "I can't hide anything from you."

"No, you never could."

"You know even if I had a crush on him, I wouldn't have hurt her."

She drew in a breath and let it out slowly. "Here's part of the problem."

"What?"

"You *did* threaten Erin, in a roundabout way."

"How?" I snapped.

"You've said you'd kill for a life like Erin had." She bit her lip. "You said it to me, days before she was killed." She gestured with her finger to encompass the kitchen. "We were right here. You were telling me how great their marriage was, and how much you envied them. It's been obvious you have a thing for Caleb. And that you really want a life like they have – had."

"You can't be serious. People say stuff like that all the time, and it doesn't mean anything." I was shaking.

She nodded slowly. "It's like the detectives said, people kill for a lot less."

"You don't think I murdered her?"

"Of course not. But I'm not the one you have to convince."

I fell back against the edge of the counter. I didn't know what to say.

"You were home alone that night?" she finally asked.

"Yes."

"Did you make any phone calls, or see the neighbors? Anything that could place you here at the house that evening."

I shook my head. "I already told the police that."

"You watched TV?"

"Yeah. *NCIS: New Orleans* was on. At least I think it was."

"You're not sure?" She pulled out her phone and tapped the screen for a minute. "That's not on on Sunday nights."

"I don't remember," I said, panic in my voice. "I don't pay attention. It's just noise to fill the silence."

She gave me a stern look. "Honey, you're going to have to pull yourself together. Who knows what the police have on you, but you can't give them more reasons to think you're lying to them."

I put my head in my hands. "I know," I said through my fingers. "You have connections with the police department, right? Can you find out what they know?"

"I'll talk to the investigators at the office, and make a few calls, but don't hold your breath." She went back to tapping the table. "I know the detectives asked you this, but is there anyone you know of who might've wanted to harm Erin?"

I shook my head. "I didn't know her that well."

But I must not have been able to completely remove the guilt from my face. She stared at me.

"What?" I asked.

"What about Rick? Did he have an affair with her? The truth."

I bit my lip. "It wouldn't surprise me."

I'd wanted to believe Caleb when he said Erin was faithful to him, but I hadn't been honest with myself.

"But you don't know?"

"No."

"You talked about their flirting. Are you sure you didn't want to see what was happening right in front of you?"

I hung my head. "I know. But would he have done that to her?"

"What would be his motive?"

"I don't know."

I told her about seeing Rick and Erin the day she'd been killed, and how their conversation had looked friendly, but then Erin had ap-peared to get mad at him.

"What was that about?" she asked.

"I don't know," I repeated. "I could ask him."

"We know he won't tell you anything, so don't even bother."

I closed my eyes. I could picture Rick doing a lot of things. Cheating on me, even with Erin, although I couldn't bring myself to think that about her. I'd built her up as too perfect. But I couldn't see Rick as a murderer.

"They're also looking at Caleb," I said.

"Of course. The husband's always a suspect. Who knows what they'll find with him."

"I've never heard of their having problems, and Caleb says things were good between them."

She tipped her head to the side and stared at me. "You talked to him?"

"Well, yes."

"Amber, you need to be very careful. I wouldn't talk to Caleb right now, to give the police any reason to think you wanted Erin out of the way so you could be with him. And, for all you know, he might have murdered her."

I swallowed hard. "He wouldn't do that."

"You don't know."

"Okay," I threw up my hands, "so what do I do now? Do I just wait to see what the police find?"

"I'll do some checking around, but you have to promise me one thing. Do not talk to the police again without me. If they come back, you call me. Promise?"

"I will. I'm scared enough, okay? I don't want to end up in jail."

She finally noticed the paperwork on the counter, both what she'd left me and what Rick had brought by. She got up and picked up the ones from Rick. She read through them, then whistled.

"Wow. Rick was really going to screw you over. I think you'll find that what I worked out is a lot more reasonable." She glanced at me. "You haven't read it yet, have you?"

I shook my head. "I just ..." My voice trailed off.

She gazed at me sadly. "I don't know why you're hesitating so much, but I'm not going to push you anymore. You do what you want to do, and I'll support you either way."

I grabbed the documents that she'd brought me the other day. "What'd you come up with for me?"

Her lips twitched into a smile. She'd known that by appearing to give up, it would prompt me to do something. She took a few minutes to explain the terms she'd come up with, and I picked up a pen. But I couldn't sign the papers.

"I just can't yet," I whispered.

She shook her head, then looked at me. "I wish you wouldn't let him do this to you."

"I know," I said. "It's just … then it really is the end of things with Rick."

"It is. And that's a good thing. It's time to let him go and move on."

I let out a dry laugh. "He said the same thing to me."

"It's true."

"And then what do I do?"

That was what my reluctance was about. Not Rick, but where I went from here.

She squeezed my hand, then gave me a quick hug. "I've got to get back to the office."

She rushed down the hall and was out the door in a flash. I stood in the kitchen and thought about what Rick had said, that he was moving on. I pictured him with Erin.

I'd ignored everything that was right in my face. Had he moved on with her? I couldn't believe Erin would do that. She was too flawless. Or maybe I was too blind. She'd been fond of Rick at one point. And as I thought about it, I realized that they'd been as friendly with each other at the barbecue as Caleb and I had been. I just hadn't noticed at the time. I shook my head. All the clues had been there, and I'd ignored them.

The quiet kept gnawing at me. I wanted to know whether Rick had been with Erin. I looked at the clock. It was 5:30. Rick usually stopped at Benjamin's Bar on Tuesday nights, after a long weekly meeting he had.

Maybe it was time to confront him.

CHAPTER ELEVEN

Benjamin's Bar was a little joint that Rick and some of his work buddies like to go to. It was downtown, the kind of place where the drinks and food were expensive, and that made the people who went there feel important. It had gotten its name not from an eponymous owner, but because the bar owner wanted to invoke a sense of money. And since Benjamin is a slang term for a hundred dollar bill, it worked as a subtle suggestion of big bucks. The bar was the cool place to go to after a day on the job, catering to a lot of Denver's business set. Now that I thought about it, it would've been the perfect place for the people in my neighborhood.

Benjamin's was crowded when I entered, lots of men and women in business casual attire, their voices raucous. I glanced around, then looked into a back room where there were more tables. Rick wasn't around. Would this be the night that he didn't show? I managed to find a seat at a small table near the rear of the main room, out of the way, where I could see Rick before he could spot me.

A waitress who seemed too young to serve alcohol approached my table and asked what I wanted to drink. I ordered a vodka tonic, then sat back and waited. The people around me looked gleeful to be out after work. A song I didn't know pounded from hidden speakers. Voices shouted to be heard over the music, and since the booze was taking effect, they became even louder.

The waitress returned a few minutes later with my drink. She asked if I wanted to run a tab, but I shook my head, not because I was anticipating leaving soon – I didn't know how long I'd be here – but because I didn't drink that much, and one vodka tonic would be plenty. I pulled some bills from my purse while she put down my drink. I paid her, and she smiled brightly at my generous tip. She sashayed off, and I sipped my drink and people-watched.

There were a lot of office types in the bar, younger career-ladder climbers who'd come here to let off some steam after a long day. Snippets of conversation drifted to me.

"… tried to tell them they didn't have it programmed right."

"I have to be in Chicago next week for the go-live …"

"He may be my boss, but he's an ass."

That last sentiment I could agree with, having had one supervisor in particular that I didn't see eye to eye with. But I found myself wistful, remembering the connections I'd had with coworkers. I'd lost all of that social contact when I'd married Rick. I'd told myself I didn't care about the career, but I wasn't sure that was true.

I spotted a couple at a table on the other side of the room. He was handsome, with a square jaw and light-colored hair. He smiled and it reminded me of Caleb. But the woman had darker hair and a fuller face, not at all like Erin. She leaned over the table, then he did as well, and they kissed, not a long, lingering kiss, but still one full of love. They were oblivious to the crowd, the noise, and the music. It was just the two of them.

It was the type of thing I'd always wanted, but when Rick and I had come here, it ended up differently. A vivid memory suddenly cut through me, one I'd hoped to forget. Rick and I had met here after work. I'd had a meeting that ran long and had arrived late. Rick was on his third drink, and he was in a mood. But as usual, he'd looked handsome in his suit, his tie loosened and slightly askew, the top button of his shirt undone, curly brown hair coming down his forehead.

We'd only been married a short time, but I'd thought I was so in love. He was a crazy guy, reckless at times. That served him well at his job; he was a deal-maker, and he was good. But he partied hard to ease his stress. That's what he told me anyway. I'd wanted that, someone to bring me out of my own shell, to keep me from being so career-focused. It was funny, I'd always said I didn't care about a career, that I wanted to marry well, as my mother had, but I hadn't found anyone, and my career had been everything. Until Rick.

Rick had thought a serious relationship – and marriage – would settle him down, and I believed that. In some ways, it had appeared as if he was reining in his hard ways, but I knew that wasn't really the case. And I had to admit that his wildness could be a turn-on. That night at the bar was a perfect example.

I'd been on edge and had just wanted to go home. He was drinking and in a wild mood. We'd fought almost immediately because he'd looked at a woman across the bar with what I'd said was a wandering eye. He, of course, denied it. I noted his drinking, and said his long hours were taking their toll. He said I needed to ease up on him, that he was working hard so we could move into the house I wanted.

As seemed to be our pattern, he was soon flirting with me, and the next thing I knew, we ended up in the bathroom. I'd said no initially, but he said it would be more fun in a public place. And I believed him. We crowded into a stall, and as he was thrusting into me, trying not to make too much noise, I kept thinking what we were risking. Someone from his office or mine could be at the bar, and they might discover us. But the danger made our lovemaking even more tantalizing, and the sex was great.

Afterward, I'd told myself this is what you did. Give them what they want, and they'll give you what you want. That was what I'd seen my mother do, and that's what I was hoping for. Rick had a great job and lots of money. We were talking about buying a house, and I'd be able to quit my job.

I was flush with the memory when Rick appeared through the crowd. I suddenly wasn't sure I could talk to him about Erin. I shifted in my chair to hide my face and tried to find some courage to go up to him.

He crossed the room to a booth and slid into the seat across from a woman sitting alone. He flashed his crazy, sexy smile, and the woman flicked her brown hair. I leaned over to get a better look at her. She was probably my age, maybe a few years younger, her shoulder-length chestnut hair very stylish, her makeup artfully applied. But the thing I immediately noticed was the big diamond ring on her left hand.

As I always seemed to do, I was going to give Rick the benefit of the doubt and assume she was a colleague, but then she reached out and laid her hand on the table. He took her hand and squeezed it, then leaned over and kissed her on the cheek. Too intimate for a work meeting.

All thoughts of talking to him were gone. I wanted to know who she was. Anger boiled up in me. He'd moved on all right, way before our divorce was official. Now I knew why he was pushing me so hard to sign the papers.

The waitress came by and he ordered, then sat back. He and his date visited, both relaxed and enjoying themselves. The waitress returned with his drink – a Manhattan, his drink of choice – and he took a big swig, then set down the glass.

He was in rare form, I thought.

I'd been the subject of his flirtations many times. When he poured on the charm, it was almost impossible to resist him. And whoever this woman was, she appeared to be falling hard for him, her smile as big as his, her laughter at just the right times in the conversation.

The music droned on, but I wasn't paying attention to the songs. I was mesmerized watching Rick carry on with another woman. Was she the same one I'd told Rick to stop seeing several months ago? As much as it hurt to admit it, I doubted she was. I couldn't see him cheating with the same woman that long. But he'd never actually said he'd break it off with that other woman, and I'd just assumed he had because his behavior had changed. I shook my head in disgust. How many women had there actually been?

I bit a fingernail. Had Erin been one of them? What would they have done if I'd walked in and found them together? And yet, I suppose Rick knew I wouldn't do that. I'd been trying too hard to be the perfect wife in the perfect neighborhood. And I couldn't see Erin doing that to Caleb. I stared at my glass as I thought of excuses. I didn't really want to know if Rick and Erin had slept together.

Rick and his date ordered another round, and drank their drinks quickly. My glass remained almost full. All the hurtful things that Rick had said and done were stuck in my throat. I could barely swallow.

A half-hour passed, and they got up. I swiveled around in my chair so they wouldn't see me, but they were too focused on each other to have noticed. She slung a leather satchel over her shoulder and flicked her hair. She wore a nice gray business suit with high heels, and she got a few looks as she headed for the door. He sidled up next to her, his hand on her ass.

I waited until they went outside, and then I hurried through the throng of people and out the door. It was dark, with a cool April chill in the air. I looked around for Rick's car, but didn't see it. Then I saw them headed up the street, and it dawned on me that he lived in the area.

They sauntered down Seventeenth Street. I let them get some distance ahead, and then I followed. I kept pace. The mall was crowded with people going to restaurants, bars, and stores, and I didn't think Rick would notice me. They turned onto Wynkoop Street, and I picked up my pace. When I reached the corner, I saw them at a side entrance to an old brick warehouse that had been turned into condos. Rick pressed numbers on a keypad, then held open the door for the woman. They disappeared inside, their laughter carrying back to me.

I crossed the street and stood in the doorway of another building. I'd done this once before, right after Rick had left me. He'd gloated as he told me he'd bought the place, which also told me he had been planning to leave me for a lot longer than I'd known. I'd stood and watched until I saw him come out onto a balcony on the third floor. With that, I'd figured out which unit was his, but at the time I hadn't known that it might be important.

Once again, I found myself watching his balcony. It was dark, but soon a rectangle of light appeared. The sliding glass doors opened, and the woman stepped onto the deck. She'd shed her jacket, exposing bare shoulders. Rick joined her, handing her a glass. They sipped their drinks for a few minutes, and then he leaned over and kissed her. It was long, and his hand went to her breast. They finally separated, then she took his hand and led him back inside.

I waited a long time in the dark, thinking one thing over and over.

He'd certainly moved on.

CHAPTER TWELVE

I lay awake that night for a long time, staring at the ceiling and thinking about Rick and this other woman. I was hurt by the fact that he was with someone else, and I was also chiding myself for how stupid I was not to believe he would. Where Erin fit into his world, I didn't know. I wondered if Rick knew the police suspected him in Erin's death. That led me to wonder: what did the police know about Rick, and what did they know about Erin? I clearly didn't really know anything about either of them.

A car drove by on the street, and a dog barked, and then it was silent. I thought back to the night Erin had been murdered. I couldn't remember what all I'd been doing. And what had Rick been doing? I needed to figure that out.

But I was also driving myself crazy thinking about the woman he'd hooked up with tonight. Who was she, and how long had she been seeing Rick? She was married, not that that made any difference to Rick. When we were dating, he'd admitted to liaisons with married women. Who was her husband, and did he suspect she was cheating on him?

I rolled on my side and punched the pillow. I wanted to know about the woman from the bar, so I figured out a plan to find out who she was. I set the alarm for five, then pulled up the covers and tried to sleep.

***

Shortly before six the next morning, I was standing across the street from Rick's condo, in the doorway to an office building. I'd desperately wanted coffee, but I didn't know when I'd be able to use the bathroom, so I'd skipped a trip to Starbucks. I yawned and rubbed my eyes, and smiled at a lone man who walked down the street. Light slowly bloomed, turning the eastern horizon amber and orange. Minutes ticked by, and gradually the sky turned a beautiful blue.

I thought about the woman from last night. She'd walked with Rick to his condo, which might mean that she had a car parked somewhere close, or that she took the light rail to and from work. Or that she lived close by. Or that she lived with him. I slapped my forehead. How could I not have thought of that? My heart raced. If that were true … no, it couldn't be. And what about the ring she wore. I'd assumed she was married, but it could be an engagement ring from Rick. Regardless, since it was Wednesday, I expected her to go to work. In a matter of minutes, she would walk out of his building, I just didn't know exactly when.

Sure enough, a little after seven, she emerged from the side entrance to Rick's building. I shrank back into the doorway and eyed her. Instead of wearing the nice gray business suit with high heels from last night, she was in tan slacks and a white blouse, with a brown coat. It was casual, but somehow she made it look elegant.

She's got clothes at his place, I thought.

This was more serious than a one-night stand. But I couldn't bring myself to believe she was living with Rick, and perhaps engaged to him. She *had* to be married to someone else. She carried the satchel that she'd had last night, and she strode quickly toward the Sixteenth Street Mall, her heels clicking loudly on the sidewalk. I stalled for a moment, and then followed from the other side of the street. She waited at the corner along with several other people for a mall shuttle bus, and I was easily able to cross the street and blend in with the crowd.

When the bus arrived, she stepped on through the front doors, and I got on at the back. She stood near the doors, a hand on a rail to keep her balance as the bus took off. I sat at the back and kept my eye on her. She took out her cell phone and started typing on it, her body swaying slightly as we barreled from street to street. When the bus stopped at Market Street, she moved around a man in a suit and hopped off the bus. Just as the back doors were closing, I stepped off. She made a beeline through a courtyard to a Starbucks.

I let another couple go through the doors and then I went inside. The woman was standing in a long line, waiting to order. The hum of voices buzzed in the air as I took a table in the corner. I pulled my phone from my purse, and pretended to check it, all the while watching her out of the corner of my eye. The baristas shouted names as they finished orders, and people would move to the counter and pick up their drinks. The woman finally ordered, then stood off to the side to wait. One of the baristas called out the name "Sarah," and she went up to the counter and took her drink. I now knew her first name.

She went back outside, took the next shuttle bus down to Curtis Street, and got off. I stepped off the bus along with a few other people and followed her up Curtis to Eighteenth. There were too many other people heading to the same building for her to be remotely suspicious of me. She crossed Eighteenth, walked down a block and to a parking lot. She went to a Silver Lexus, opened the trunk, then rifled through a box. She pulled out some manila files and put them in her bag, closed the trunk, and headed back down Eighteenth. She entered the south tower of the Denver Place building, a tall, two-tower office skyscraper with an expansive breezeway that connected the two buildings. She went to a bank of elevators and got on.

I hesitated, but when two men who were chatting about a ballgame went to the elevator, I made my move and joined them. Sarah stood by the door, her coffee cup in one hand, her cell phone magically appearing in the other. She never once looked up, but adroitly typed on her phone with her thumb. She was unaware of the men talking, or of me. The elevator stopped on the twenty-fifth floor, and she was the only one who got off.

At this point, if I got off, I risked her recognizing me from the Starbucks or on the mall shuttle, so I stayed on the elevator. But I was able to peek out before the doors slid closed. Sarah went to the left.

I rode the elevator up to twenty-eight, and got off with the two men. I waited until they went into an office on the right, and then I pushed the button for an elevator going down. When it came, I rode to twenty-five and got off. A sign that I hadn't seen before pointed to two offices on the left, for McMillan and Cohen, Attorneys at Law, and Arrow Tech. The law office was familiar, but I wasn't sure why. I made note of both companies, then rode back down to the lobby.

I went around the corner to the breezeway that connected the two buildings. Several tables, chairs, and booths made a nice sitting area near the stores and restaurants. I went into one and ordered a ham and cheese croissant and a large latte, then took that to a booth and sat down.

While I relished my small meal, I took out my phone and looked up Arrow Tech. It was the trend these days to include employee bios and even pictures, but I didn't see Sarah on their website, so I looked up

McMillan and Cohen. Then it dawned on me where I'd seen that name. It was on the paperwork Rick had left. The food in my stomach curdled.

Is that how he met Sarah?

I poked around the website until I found a listing of the firm's employees. And there was a professional photo of Sarah in a business suit, law books behind her. Her last name was Papin, and she was an associate lawyer. She'd been at the firm for two years, and she specialized in family law. Which probably meant divorce work as well. I sat back. Rick's lawyer was a man, but I wondered why he hadn't used Sarah as his attorney?

I stared at her photo. How long had she been seeing Rick? Knowing him, they could've been dating for months, and then when he decided to divorce me, it had been easy to find a lawyer at her office. A slow rage rose in me. At that moment, I could've killed Rick. But then, perhaps for the first time in my entire life, I knew I needed to look inward.

A lot of that anger needed to be directed at myself. I'd let him do all those things to me. The drunken fights, the threats. The cheating. I hadn't put up my hand and said enough. It was just like my mother had done. I know she'd had suspicions about my father, just as I had. Had he been a philanderer? But like my mother apparently had done, I'd dismissed those thoughts about him as soon as they'd arisen. I didn't want to think that about my father. Yet the doubts remained. My mother had accepted it as a trade-off for the lifestyle she wanted. And she had seemed happy enough with her life, so I didn't worry. Now I was realizing that, when it was your own husband, it wasn't such an easy thing to dismiss. At least not for me.

I was tempted to call Sarah right now, but I didn't know what I'd say to her. I stared at my phone. Then it occurred to me that she was in family law. There was my in. I found the number for McMillan and Cohen and dialed it. A moment later, a woman crisply answered.

"I'd like to speak to Sarah Papin," I said.

"May I ask who's calling?"

"Carol Farenstein."

I had no idea where the name had come from, it just popped into my head.

"One moment."

A couple of clicks sounded, and then a voice said, "Sarah Papin."

Her voice was low and commanding, the kind that reminded me of Bette Davis or some other old film star. The kind that I'm sure Rick thought was sensual.

I hesitated. "I'm in the middle of getting a divorce, and a friend of a friend recommended you."

"Oh, who was that?"

"It was ... Jessica Samuelson." I wasn't very good at this lying thing.

"I don't know who that is."

"Unfortunately my soon-to-be ex is getting irritated with me," I went on. That certainly was true. "I'm wondering if you might have some time to meet me today. I've got to get things moving forward."

"I'm sorry, but I don't. I've got appointments all day, but I could meet you ..." In the background, papers flipped. She still used some kind of day calendar that probably sat on her desk. "It looks like I have time tomorrow morning. Say ten o'clock?"

"Sure, let's book it."

"Your name again?"

I hesitated, panicked because I wasn't sure what I'd told her. "Carol Farenstein," I finally said.

"Great. Let me put you down. What's your phone number?"

I rattled off a fake number.

"Perfect, I'll see you then."

I thanked her, and the line went dead.

CHAPTER THIRTEEN

I sat for a long time, thinking about my own duplicity, but that desperate need to know more about this woman overrode any guilt I might've had. She was busy for the day – or at least that's what she'd told me. What should I do now? I could leave and come back, but what if I missed her? I decided to stay put. I'd left my car in a lot down near Rick's condo, and I didn't have to worry about paying for parking or getting ticketed or towed until after midnight.

The lobby was quiet. I got back on my phone and went to LinkedIn, where I looked up Sarah Papin. She'd done her undergraduate studies at the University of Ohio, and then law school at Pepperdine School of Law in Malibu. Not bad. She was a smart cookie. She did an internship at a law firm in San Jose, and when I looked up the firm, it appeared to be fairly prestigious, based on the articles that came up with my search. I checked her graduation dates and guessed her to be about twenty-nine, so she really was a new lawyer. That put her about five years younger than Rick and I.

She belonged to a few attorneys' associations, and she was part of the Pepperdine Alumni Association. The picture she'd used for LinkedIn was the same one as the law firm's. She appeared to be lining up her career very nicely.

That's exactly how I had been at one time. But for me, it was only a bridge until I could find the right man, get married, and settle down. I snorted. Like Rick was the right man. How wrong I had been.

I continued to research Sarah. Her Facebook page had a lot of pictures, but unlike Erin, Sarah utilized her privacy settings better and I couldn't find out much more about her. I scrolled through the pictures. In several, she was with a man about her age who had short, curly blond hair. In one, they were on a beach, with a gorgeous sunset behind them, both with wide grins. In another, they were at a restaurant. Her husband? I tried to find a name for him, but she'd never posted that.

I looked for more social media accounts for Sarah, but couldn't find any. I did find a few papers that she contributed to, discussing aspects of family law. I read through them, learned nothing significant, and was bored in the process. I suddenly became aware that the lobby was growing more crowded, people going back and forth between the two towers. I glanced at the time. It was already noon.

My stomach growled. I put my phone away, stood up, and walked around until I found a bathroom and freshened up, then got a bite to eat at a Quiznos. I took my lunch and sat at a booth where I was hidden but could still see people walking by. A while later, Sarah went into the restaurant near the Starbucks. She emerged a few minutes later with a Styrofoam container. Getting her lunch to go. Too much to do. I'd bet the law firm kept her busy. Kristen had kept crazy hours when she first started at her firm, and it hadn't let up much in the years since.

Sarah went right back to the bank of elevators, headed back upstairs. I finished my lunch, walked around for a while, and then took up a spot in a different place. I spent some time reading my Kindle book, but I wasn't connecting to the story, and I set my phone down. I stared into space, thinking about Rick and Sarah. He was pushing me to move on. Was it because he wanted to pursue something with her? If she was married – surely she was – she'd have to get a divorce first. And what about Erin? Had Rick been seeing her at some point, too? I let out a huge sigh filled with contempt for him.

My phone rang and I snatched it up. It was Kristen.

"Hey," I said.

"What's all that noise? Where are you?" she immediately asked, her voice suspicious. She knew I rarely went out these days.

"Just running some errands."

I decided I wasn't going to tell her about my spying. She'd only think I was crazy to interfere with the police investigation. And maybe I was.

"Have you found out what the police know about Erin's murder?" I asked.

"No. They're being pretty tightlipped, at least from what my investigators said. I'll keep on it, but in the meantime, did you know the McCormicks are having financial trouble?"

"What? I don't know anything about that. What's going on?"

"It's true. Apparently Caleb's business hasn't been doing well. They're behind on their bills, and I'd say things look pretty bleak for them."

"How do you know this?"

"I asked the investigators to check."

"Oh," I said. "What's Caleb's business?"

"He owns some kind of financial company. You didn't know?"

"No. I remember him talking to Rick when we had them over for that barbecue, but I didn't pay any attention."

"You were too enamored with his looks."

"Ha ha," I said, but she'd hit the mark. I'd never paid attention to what Caleb did, I just watched him go to and from work. And I'd always assumed he and Erin had money to spare. I sucked in a breath. "They'll think Caleb did it."

"You got it. And for all you know, he did."

"No way."

"Amber, just because you've built up this great picture of him in your mind, don't think he couldn't do something like that to his wife so he could get his hands on the insurance money."

"All right. I've got to go, okay? Thanks for letting me know."

"Sure," she said slowly, as if questioning why I was brushing her off. "I'll talk to you later."

I ended the call, and immediately got back on the Internet. I googled Caleb McCormick and found his business. It looked like many other businesses, but from a website you wouldn't be able to tell if the company was successful or not. I found his picture on the "About Us" section. He looked handsome – as usual – and every bit the powerful CEO of the company. Everything I thought he was.

My thoughts drifted to Erin. If they were having money troubles, why was she continuing in her lifestyle? Wouldn't that be the time to cut back? Unless she didn't know about the money trouble. I couldn't believe that Caleb would keep secrets from her. That wasn't him, I told myself, although I really didn't have any idea what they spoke about. I put my phone down, more confused than ever. I hadn't known about the McCormicks' money troubles.

It was three o'clock, and in order to follow Sarah after work, I needed to get my car. I went to the restroom again, then strode outside and walked at a brisk pace to Sixteenth Street. I was too focused to notice how nice a day it was, the sun out, the temperature pleasant. I took a shuttle to the lot where my car was, then returned to the Denver Place complex and found a metered spot across from the south tower entrance. I listened to music on the radio and watched the building. Traffic built up, and I wished again for some coffee. It had been a long day.

Shortly before five, I donned sunglasses and a white hat I wore when I golfed. It wasn't much of a disguise, but it would do. Finally, at six o'clock, Sarah came out of the building and stood at the corner. I waited to see what she'd do. If she walked to a bar or restaurant, or to Rick's, I'd get out and follow on foot. If she took her car, I hoped I could maneuver through the rush-hour traffic and keep up with her.

The light changed and Sarah crossed Curtis Street. I had to wait for traffic to pass, but then I pulled into a lane and drove down the next block. Sarah was halfway into the intersection. By the time I pulled to the curb near the parking lot, she was at her car. She put her satchel in the backseat, then got in and drove out of the lot. I fell in behind her.

We meandered through downtown. I did what I'd read about in detective novels, and let a few cars get between hers and mine, but since traffic was heavy and slow, I didn't worry about losing her. She made it to Broadway and headed north. She soon came to Interstate 70, which was packed with rush-hour traffic, and went east. She was moving faster now, but I still had no trouble keeping the Lexus in sight. A half-hour later, her car turned onto Peña Boulevard.

She's going to the airport. To go out of town or to pick someone up?

Traffic was lighter, and she hit seventy miles per hour. I kept some distance between us, but could easily see her car on the highway. She eventually went to the west terminal and drove to the underground level for arrivals. The car slowed at the United area. A man with curly blond hair stood in a blue suit without a tie. A carry-on bag sat next to him. The Lexus pulled to the curb and he opened the passenger door, put his bag in the back seat, and got in.

I noticed him give her a peck on the cheek, but that was the extent of their affections. No embrace of any kind, let alone something more passionate. The Lexus took off, with me tailing. They drove from Peña Boulevard to Interstate 225. We went south and then west, and ended up on Belleview. The Lexus eventually turned onto Berry Avenue. At that point, I slowed down. If I turned now, I was certain Sarah would realize she'd been followed. A car horn blared at me, and I went around the corner and parked.

The Lexus had pulled into the driveway of a two-story house with a large evergreen tree in front. The headlights hit the garage door as it went up, and the car disappeared inside. The door closed. I waited a long time, giving Sarah and the man enough time to get inside and occupy themselves with whatever they did in the evening, and then I drove down the street. I slowed down and noted the house number as I went by, then continued to the end of the block. I turned onto the next street and stopped. I grabbed my phone and googled their address, then looked up some search results in some people-search sites. Based on the address, it took me a few minutes, but I found out that Sarah was married to James Papin. He was two years older than she was.

I sat back and stared at my phone. I had a decent amount of information on Sarah Papin. She wasn't engaged to Rick. She was a married lawyer who worked at McMillan and Cohen downtown. But she was having an affair with one of her firm's clients, who also happened to be my estranged husband.

I just didn't know what to do with that information yet.

CHAPTER FOURTEEN

After a few more minutes of staring into the darkness, I drove around the block and back by Sarah's house. There was a light on in an upstairs window. What was going on in there? James was probably filling her in about his trip. Did he have any inkling about what she'd been doing while he was gone? I didn't know, and it didn't matter. I'd found out what I'd wanted to about Sarah. It had been a long day and I was ready to go home.

I headed back to my house, which wasn't too far west of Sarah's place. It was dark and quiet as I drove down my block. There were no lights on at the McCormick house, although Caleb could've been in the back of the house and I wouldn't have been able to tell.

I pulled into my garage, turned off the car, and shut the garage door. I grabbed my purse and trudged into the house, then flicked on the lights in the kitchen. The house was cold and quiet. Depressing. What should I do for dinner? I was hungry, but too tired to think. The doorbell sounded and made me jump.

Who was coming over at this hour? Rick?

I went down the shadowy hall to the front door and looked out the peephole. A dark figure stood on the porch. I couldn't tell if it was Rick. I hesitated, then turned on the porch light and peered into the peephole again. Caleb was blinking at the sudden light. I flung open the door.

"Hi, Caleb. What's going on?" I was too cheery.

His face was drawn, the stubble on his cheeks giving him a swarthy look.

"Do you have a few minutes?" he asked. "I need to talk to someone."

"Sure. Come on in."

I stepped back. As he passed by me, I smelled booze on his breath. I was more than familiar with that smell on a man. Too many times Rick had come home reeking. I glanced outside. Across the street, a light was on in Tiffany's front window. I thought I saw movement behind the sheer curtains. I shut the door, but if Tiffany had seen Caleb, it was too late.

Caleb started for the living room.

"Would you like a drink?" I asked, then regretted it. He'd probably had enough, but to offer was the social convention, and I didn't know what else to say.

"Sure. Scotch?"

"I think I've got some."

He took a seat on the couch, and I hurried into the kitchen. I found a bottle of Johnnie Walker that Rick had left and poured a small amount into a glass.

"Ice?" I called out.

"Yes."

I got ice from the refrigerator, then took the glass and returned to the living room. Caleb was gazing at the floor. I handed him the glass, then sat on the loveseat.

"What's going on?" I asked.

He took a drink and let out a sigh. "Man, it's been a long day."

I could relate, but I kept my mouth shut. He took another swig and stared at the glass. The ice swirled around, and he seemed mesmerized by it.

"I had to go to the funeral home today." He shook his head, bewildered. "I never thought I'd be dealing with this now."

"Do you need me to do anything?"

"No. Erin's mom and sister are helping out and guiding things. You wouldn't believe all the stuff you have to deal with. What kind of service do you want? What kind of music should be played? Is there anyone who wants to do a eulogy? Who will be the pallbearers? It doesn't end."

He lapsed into silence, and I sat quietly, aching for him.

"The police came back today," he went on, then took another drink, but realized it was only ice, so he set the glass down on the coffee table.

"What did they want?"

"You're not going to believe this, but I'm sure they think I had something to do with Erin's death."

I played dumb. "Why is that?"

"I told you I have a life insurance policy on her, and she had one on me. A million dollars each. The thing is, I wouldn't do anything to her."

"Why would the police think you need the money?" If they were on the verge of bankruptcy, that's why, I left unsaid. I was curious to see if he'd tell me about his money problems, but I didn't want him to know I'd found out things about him behind his back.

He drew in a breath. "Unfortunately, my business has been

struggling lately."

"You're in finance?"

He smiled. "You remembered."

I licked my lips and smiled back. As if I recalled that from last summer. Right.

"Yes, I'm in finance and investing. Things were going along well, but I think I should've done a few things differently here and there that I didn't. And the company's paying for it now."

I stared at him, wondering about this man who I thought couldn't make a wrong move. And now he was admitting that he had. I don't know why it shocked me, but it did.

He ran his hands over his face. "I don't know what to do. Money was tight at home, too. Ah, maybe I shouldn't tell you that."

"It's okay," I murmured.

That seemed to mollify him.

He ran a hand over his face. "The truth is, the past few months, I tried to get Erin to stop spending so much, but she wouldn't. She liked to golf, and the health club was important to her. And she liked going out with her friends." He hesitated saying the last sentence, maybe realizing I hadn't been one of Erin's friends. "And I liked her doing those things. Besides, I didn't tell her how bad things really were, so how would she know?"

"Why didn't you tell her?"

He glanced away. "It would only upset her."

"But if it was putting you in a bind …"

He didn't say anything to that. "The thing is, we haven't filed for bankruptcy, we just have a lot of debt. But I can pull the business up again. I've been working long hours to make it happen. And I work at home almost every night. But the company's going to turn a corner, and things will be better. It's just a rough time for Erin and me, financially speaking. That doesn't mean I would kill her and get the insurance money. The police can talk to the guys working for me. They know how hard we've all been working, and where things are heading."

"You were at home the night Erin …"

He nodded miserably. "Yes. And I don't have an alibi."

"Erin didn't know how bad things were?"

"She knew some, in the last couple of weeks, but not that we're close to bankruptcy. I'd told her I wanted her to cut back. And I was saying I wanted our finances in order since we were going to have kids soon. I know it wasn't the best time to start a family, but I was pushing it because I thought that would make her happier."

I thought again of Erin's Facebook post, and how she didn't seem ready to have a family anytime soon.

"That's not usually what happens," I said. "Babies are challenging."

"I don't know. I thought it'd be good."

"Have the police figured out anything?"

"They're not telling me a thing. They just keep asking questions about our relationship, trying to pin her murder on me."

"Have you talked to Tiffany or Melissa? Do they know anything?"

"Nothing's changed. They don't know what Erin was doing that day or why she was found near that motel."

What if I ask them? They might share with someone else things they wouldn't share with Caleb. But those two women wouldn't likely talk to me. Was it even worth trying? Or maybe Kayla could ask those questions. I could talk to her tomorrow. Right now, I was having a hard time keeping my eyes open. As much as I wanted to spend the time with Caleb, I was exhausted. I stifled a yawn. I'd been up early, and I hadn't slept well last night. Caleb must've noticed because he got up.

"I've taken too much of your time."

"It's okay." I pushed myself up.

"I appreciate you talking to me," he said as we walked to the door. "The other women, they're nice, but ..." He smiled. "Seeing you every day in the window, I feel like I know you. It sounds crazy."

"It's not," I whispered.

"I'll see you tomorrow."

He opened the door and stepped onto the porch. I waved and he headed down the sidewalk and crossed the street. I turned out the porch light and shut the door, then headed upstairs and went to bed.

I'd deal with Rick, Sarah, and everything else tomorrow.

CHAPTER FIFTEEN

The next morning I wasn't looking out the window. I didn't have time. I had to get up and get ready for my appointment with Sarah Papin, and even though I may have felt it, I wanted to look anything but the despondent wife. I wanted Sarah to know that the previous competition had been something. I'd been something before I'd given up my job. I hadn't always been the frumpy housewife that I somehow had become.

I showered, then found a light gray business suit in the closet. I couldn't remember the last time I'd worn it. I took it off the hanger, but I needed to press a green silk blouse to go with it. Once that was completed, I put on makeup, doing myself up well. I dug my high heels out of the back of my closet and I even put on some sleek gold earrings that my mother had given me for my last birthday. I'd hardly worn them because they were too dressy for any occasions I had.

Getting ready took longer than I thought it would, and when I finished, I surveyed myself in the mirror. I looked good. Better, in fact, than I had in a long time. I smiled, and that felt good. When I worked, I frequently dressed like this – maybe without these particular earrings – and I'd felt like I could handle anything. I had the talent, but the suit and heels did help.

I went downstairs, fixed a cup of coffee, then stood in the kitchen and sipped it. My hand shook slightly. Was I crazy to be doing what I was about to do? I shook my head. Who knew? I finally put my cup in the sink and headed to the garage. As I was backing out, I saw Kayla from next door. She was walking down the sidewalk with a stroller. She waited for me to back into the street. Then I rolled down my window.

"Don't you look good?" she said with a smile.

"Thanks."

"Are you back to work?"

I shook my head. "I've got a meeting."

"A job interview?"

"No, nothing like that." I glanced across the street. No one was around. "Hey," I said to Kayla. "Do you talk to Tiffany and Melissa much?"

"Some. Why?"

"Do you know what they said to the police? Caleb was asking, and I didn't know how to answer."

"Oh." She frowned. "I haven't talked to them since the day Erin died. They're both pretty upset about what happened. It's still such a shock."

"Yes."

We chatted for a minute longer, and then I told her I needed to get going. She waved as I drove down the street. It was cool and gray out, and a light rain fell. I drove in silence, and by the time I got downtown, the rain had stopped, leaving the streets and sidewalks covered with a wet sheen. I parked and walked to the Denver Place south tower, then rode the elevator up to the McMillan and Cohen offices. My stomach was a knot of nerves.

I got off the elevator and entered through a glass door. A

receptionist looked up at me with a thin smile.

"May I help you?" she asked in a prim voice.

"I have a ten o'clock appointment with Sarah Papin." My hand went to fix my collar, even though it didn't need adjustment.

She glanced at her computer monitor. "I'll let her know you're here. Would you like to have a seat?"

I sat down on a leather couch as she picked up a phone and murmured into it. Then she quietly replaced it and looked at me.

"She'll be with you in a moment."

"Thank you."

I picked up a copy of the *Denver Post*, and as I thumbed through the newspaper, the words didn't register. I kept thinking I should leave before I got too far into this charade. I crossed my leg, my foot tapping the table. Ten minutes later, Sarah Papin strode into the lobby.

"I'm so sorry to keep you waiting," she said.

I stood up and she shook my hand and introduced herself. She was in a tan pencil skirt and simple blue blouse, but she somehow made it look professional. I was glad I'd dressed up.

"I was on a call, and it ran a little long." She waved a hand. "Come down to my office."

She escorted me down a short hall and into a corner office that had a stunning view of the Rocky Mountains.

Not bad for a newbie lawyer, I thought to myself.

"Have a seat," she said.

She pointed to a wingback chair across from a mahogany desk. She shut the door and took a seat at a large desk chair, then leaned forward.

"So," she said, "your husband wants a divorce."

"That's right."

She picked up a yellow legal pad and pen, then leaned back and crossed a leg, resting the pad on her thigh. She looked up at me expectantly.

"We've been separated for about six months," I began. I watched to see if that drew any reaction. It didn't, so I continued. "He's a decent guy, he's got a good job in pharmaceutical sales, but he definitely has a wild streak."

She took notes, and if it occurred to her that I might be talking about Rick, she was good at not showing it.

"He's been pushing me to get the divorce finalized, so he can move on." She glanced at me and nodded. "But the truth is, he already has."

"Oh?" she murmured.

"He's already with another woman, and there may have been others while we were married."

"That's in your favor."

"Is it?"

She glanced up at me. "It leaves him in less of a bargaining position, if you want to make things difficult for him."

I took a long time to reply. "Maybe."

She wrote something down, and then said, "I didn't catch what your husband's name is."

"Rick Aldridge."

The pen stopped. "I'm sorry. You told me your name is Carol Farenstein."

"I did."

She stared at me. "You're ..." Words failed her.

"Amber."

Our eyes locked for several long seconds, and then she put the pad and pen on the desk.

"I think this meeting is over." Her voice warbled.

I held up a hand. "Not so fast."

She sucked in a breath through her teeth. "You need to leave."

"Not until we talk."

She reached for the phone.

"If you call security," I said in a threatening tone, "I'll make such a scene, you'll wish you'd never met Rick, or me."

She stared at me for a long time, her hand poised above the phone. She finally laid her hand on the desk. "I've only been with Rick after he left you, if that's what you want to know."

"Isn't that nice. You're still married, though."

Her jaw dropped. "That's none of your business."

"Maybe not, but I want to know this: were you with Rick on Sunday night?"

"I don't know. I'd … have to think."

"A storm came through, and it rained for a bit." I pointed at the day calendar on her desk. "Why don't you look there? It might refresh your memory."

She held my gaze for a moment, then pulled the calendar over and flipped through it. "Oh, yes. That night. I had a dinner engagement with my husband. It was a conference that lasted until after ten. Then we went home."

"You weren't with Rick at all that night?"

Confusion flickered in her eyes. "No." Then she tacked on, "There were other couples there. They'd remember me."

"Maybe I should ask them. Or your husband."

"Leave him out of this," she hissed.

"Well, let's see if you answer all my questions."

"Why are you doing this to me?"

"It's not you. You just happened to be with Rick."

"What do you care about what he does? You're separated. He's going to divorce you, if you'll ever sign the damn paperwork."

He'd been talking to her about me.

"He can't stand you," she went on. "He thinks you're weak."

That stung, but I moved on. "Were you with Rick seven or eight months ago?"

"No," she said forcefully.

I narrowed my eyes. "That's the truth?"

Her hands were shaking, and she planted them on the desk. "Yes. I've only been seeing him for a month or two. He's been out of your house long before that. Why are you worried about what he's doing? He doesn't love you."

"You think he loves you?"

She didn't say anything to that.

I debated telling her about the police, and their questions about Rick. But I knew she'd tell him, and I didn't want that just yet.

"I don't know what you want." Her voice rose, angry and defensive. "But I'm telling you now, I never saw Rick while he was married to you."

"Be careful," I warned her, "or I'll talk to your husband."

She paled, but she managed to glare at me.

"Who else was Rick seeing?" I asked.

Her eyebrows shot up, as if it hadn't occurred to her that Rick might be seeing someone besides her. "Why don't you ask him? He obviously wasn't getting satisfied with you, so he looked elsewhere."

I ignored that. We fell into a staring contest.

"How did you find out about us?" she finally asked.

"It wasn't too hard. If you know where Rick likes to drink – and I do – then it was a matter of going there. And you were with him. It was easy to see it wasn't a business engagement. If I found you that easily, your husband could, too."

She turned red. "My husband doesn't know anything about this, and it better stay that way."

"We'll see."

I stood up and went to the door. "If I find out you know more than you're telling me ..."

"About what?"

That was the question.

"You think you'll leave your husband for Rick? Trust me, you'll have your hands full."

She was looking at her legal pad as I opened the door and stepped into the hall. I walked back to the reception area.

"Have a nice day," the receptionist said as I passed by.

"You, too," I called over my shoulder as I went out the door.

I had a feeling both of us would have a better day than Sarah. Or Rick.

CHAPTER SIXTEEN

I hurried to the elevator and got on. Two men were discussing a software programming problem, and I faced the door, my heart pounding. We rode down to the lobby and I went into the breezeway, but stopped where I could see the elevators. I waited a minute to see if Sarah Papin emerged. When she didn't, I rushed to my car, got in, and locked the doors. I sat for a full minute. My hands were shaking, so I grabbed the steering wheel.

On the one hand, I couldn't believe that I'd had the nerve to confront Sarah like that. On the other hand, I couldn't believe that she wasn't the woman that Rick had been seeing before he'd moved out. She'd been adamant that they'd only been seeing each other for a short time. I tended to believe her. But that left the question of who Rick had been seeing while we were still married. An ugly thought crept into my mind. Had it been Erin? I bit my lip. No way.

My mind was racing, so I took in a few deep breaths to calm down, then glanced up at the silver Denver Place tower. I thought Sarah might leave and confront Rick, but she was probably on the phone with him right now. He'd be furious about what I did. I wondered how long it would take before he'd come to the house to confront me. I knew he would, and I wasn't looking forward to it. But he was usually busy at work, so I doubted he'd be able to get away before lunch, and maybe not even then. It would be better if I weren't around the house for a while. I wanted to be in something more comfortable, though. I glanced down at my nice suit. It had been too long since I'd worn business attire and heels all day long.

More people were hustling along the streets, going to lunch, as I jammed the key in the ignition and fired up my Beemer. I waited for a lull in traffic, then pulled onto Eighteenth Street and headed home. I turned into my driveway and into the garage, but before I could shut the door, Kayla appeared.

"Hey, Amber," she said. Her smile was forced. "How'd your meeting go?"

"Just fine," I replied. I hoped my voice wasn't warbling because I still felt fire in my nerves.

"That's good to hear." She glanced around, and shifted from foot to foot like a nervous child. "I talked to Melissa after you left."

"Oh?" I tried for nonchalant.

"She said you should stay away from Caleb, that he's got enough to deal with right now."

"I haven't been bugging him," I said a bit defensively. "He popped over last night to talk to me, and I went to his house one day to offer my condolences, but that's it."

The moment the words were out of my mouth, I regretted them. I shouldn't have let her – or anyone else – know when I'd seen Caleb. It was none of their business, and I didn't need Tiffany or Melissa knowing what I'd done.

"That's all I did," I finished.

She tipped her head. "You've somehow made Melissa mad. She

said that Erin threatened you to stay away from Caleb."

I shrugged. "That's not what happened."

She searched my face. "Okay. I wanted to let you know. Anyway, I have to get back inside." She waved a hand. "You have a great afternoon."

With that, she spun around and hurried across the grass to her house.

What was going on with Melissa, I thought as I listened to the garage door hum closed.

I went into the kitchen. My stomach was growling, so I grabbed a few cookies and washed them down with some milk. I could grab a bite later, but I needed to get changed and leave before Rick showed up. I put my glass in the sink, dashed upstairs, and changed into jeans and a blouse. It was still cool, so I grabbed a light jacket, then thought to get my laptop. I took those and my purse, threw them in the passenger seat of the car, and opened the garage door. I got in and backed onto the driveway. I reached up and had just pressed the remote when I heard the squeal of tires on pavement.

I glanced in the rearview mirror. Rick's blue Lexus was blocking the driveway. I looked around frantically, not sure what to do. I'd dawdled too long while he'd raced here. I hit the remote again and the garage door slowly opened. I pulled into the garage, but before I could get out, Rick appeared in my window.

"We need to talk, Amber," he shouted.

I hit the door lock and then stared straight ahead at peeling drywall tape at the front of the garage.

Go away, I thought desperately.

He rapped with his knuckles on the window. "Get out. Now."

I finally mustered the courage to look at him. "You need to go away!"

"You had no business talking to Sarah."

"Yes, I did."

He tried to wrench open the door, then pulled at the handle in frustration. "Open this!"

"You need to calm down."

He glared at me. I looked in the rearview mirror, thinking Tiffany or Melissa or Kayla might hear the commotion and come out. None of them did. How come when I needed them to be paying attention to me, they weren't?

He stepped back and crossed his arms. "Why'd you talk to Sarah?"

I contemplated him for a moment, then cracked the window. "I needed to know."

"Know what?"

"What went on between you and Erin?" I glowered at him. His eyes darted around. "Don't lie to me."

"What does that have to do with Sarah?"

"Tell me!"

He stepped back and then threw up his hands. "All right. You want to hear I had an affair with Erin? Fine. I did."

I gazed up at him, so disappointed, but not entirely with him. Erin deserved some of it. With all that she had, I couldn't believe she would do that to me.

"How long did it last?" I asked.

"Not very long. A couple of months."

"Is she the one? When you came home and I was in bed?"

He knew exactly what I meant. The night when I'd told him it had to stop. He didn't say anything, and I knew right then there had been other women besides Erin.

I stared at him. "How many?"

He shrugged. "Does it matter?"

"Why did you do this to me?"

It took him a moment to answer. "I knew it was the wrong thing soon after we got married." He reached out and tapped the window. "And so did you. You knew we weren't right for each other. I know you thought I'd settle down, and maybe I did, too. But … I *like* the fast lane. And you didn't want to be there with me. You never wanted to *do* anything." He waved a hand around. "This house, this lifestyle … it's never been me. I should've known that long before, but I didn't."

"That didn't mean you had to sleep with a bunch of women."

He gave me a cocky smile, just as he'd done when I'd first met him. At the time, he'd seemed so cool. Now I wanted to throw up.

He shrugged. "That's just who I am. And as far as Sarah is concerned, you know damn well that you and I are separated, and we're not going to get back together."

His voice rose. "Why'd you go see her?"

"I wanted to know if you were seeing her while we were still married."

"I wasn't," he snarled.

I nodded slowly, sadly. "I also needed to know what you were doing that night."

"When?" Then it dawned on him what I meant. "The night Erin was killed? That's why you were asking Sarah what she was doing that night? And what I was doing?"

"Yes."

"What do you care?"

"The police were asking about you."

"Why?"

I shrugged. "They must suspect something."

He took a step back and glanced out into the street.

"I saw you the day she died," I said. "You stopped by the house and wanted me to sign the papers, remember? But when you were driving off, Erin was taking a walk. You stopped and she came over to your car. You two talked. At first she seemed okay, but then she got mad at you. What was that about?"

He couldn't look me in the eye. "Nothing."

"Did you ever meet her at the Standard Motel?"

"No."

I could tell he was lying.

"That's where she was discovered. Near there."

"I know that," he said a bit too abruptly.

"Why do the police think you're involved?" I repeated.

"I don't know."

"Were you at the motel that day?"

He shook his head.

"What were you doing the night she was killed?"

"It's none of your business."

"You know, Rick, I could be the only person that might defend you."

His eyes narrowed. "I was with another woman," he finally said.

"Not Sarah?"

He didn't say a word.

I snorted. "You're sleeping around on Sarah, too? Does she have any idea?"

"How should I know? I told you this is none of your business."

Somewhere the tables had turned, and instead of his being angry and threatening with me, he was the one backed into a corner.

"Do you have any idea why Erin would've been around that motel if she wasn't there to see you?" I asked.

"How do you know she was at the motel?"

"I don't."

He frowned. "If she went there, she could've been there with any guy, not just me."

My jaw dropped. "What do you mean?"

"You think I'm the only one she was sleeping with?"

"That's not true," I said.

"You may have thought she was perfect and wonderful, but trust me, that wasn't the case."

I stared at that damn peeling tape on the wall and shook my head. "That can't be. Don't lie about her when she's gone and can't defend herself. She wouldn't do that to Caleb."

"But she did." He frowned at me. "Oh, man. What you don't know."

"Does Caleb know?"

"No. He adored her, and she walked circles around him. He was passive … kind of like you."

"You call him 'passive.' I call him a good man."

He laughed. "Whatever."

"Did you know they were having financial trouble? But he was working hard to give her everything she wanted."

He sighed. "Maybe that wasn't enough." He stared down at me

with such cold and angry eyes, it was frightening. He tapped the window again. "Stay away from Sarah, and don't interfere in my life anymore. Sign those papers from my lawyer and finalize this divorce. You hear me?"

I stared up at him. I was scared. He turned and walked down the driveway to his car. He got in, gunned the engine, and the car roared off down the street. I sat and looked out the windshield for a long time.

CHAPTER SEVENTEEN

I finally got out of the car and stood in the garage. I was shaking as I started toward the door. Then another voice startled me.

"Amber?"

I whirled around, thinking Rick had somehow returned. But it was Caleb. I tried to regain my composure.

"Are you okay?" he said as he stared at me.

"I'm … fine," I replied slowly.

He glanced toward the driveway, then back at me. "Was Rick just here?"

I nodded.

His brow furrowed. "Are you sure you're all right?"

"Yes."

He grew serious. "Hey, I wanted to talk to you about something."

"Oh?" I leaned against the hood of the car.

"I saw the garage door open, so I …" He hesitated and looked around. "I was talking to Tiffany this morning …"

"This can't be good," I muttered.

"You … uh … wouldn't have … Were you mad at Erin … enough to …" He left the rest unsaid.

My jaw dropped. "Caleb, how could you say that? I would never do something like that to you … or Erin."

He stared at me, his eyes growing cool. "Tiffany told me an interesting story."

"Oh?" I waited for him to go on, and I suddenly knew what he was going to tell me.

"Tiffany said that shortly after you moved into the neighborhood, you asked her for a health club recommendation," he went on. "She told you about the place that she and Melissa and Erin went to. So you started going there, too, and Tiffany said one time you were there, after you'd been working out, you told her how much you'd wanted to be in this neighborhood, and you were so happy you found the house you moved into. You said it was important to you, and how much you wanted this," he waved a hand around, "kind of life."

I gulped but stayed quiet.

"Tiffany also said another time Erin was there, and she was talking about when she and I had gone to Fiji, and how she'd given up her job when we got married and how she was loving her life. Then after Erin walked away," he pointed a finger at me, "you told Tiffany you'd *kill* for that life."

I gaped at him, stunned, but he was serious.

"That's just something people say," I said. My mouth was dry. "You must know that's not something I would act on."

"But Erin's dead." His voice was flat. "And Tiffany–"

I started to protest, and he held up a hand.

"Of course I know that normally, a person wouldn't do that, but Tiffany said that all along, she's known that you were really jealous of Erin, and me, and what we have. And that you wanted it." He narrowed his eyes. "Not only that, Tiffany said it became pretty obvious that as your marriage fell apart, you were looking at me." He hesitated. "That you wanted me."

I couldn't find the words to argue. I didn't want to lie to him. The reality was that what he was saying was the truth. I did want Caleb, and I would've left Rick for Caleb, if he would've had me. But that's not what happened.

"Caleb, you don't understand," I said. "It's not like that."

"What is it like?"

An image of my mother came to mind. "Ever since I was a kid, I thought this," and I waved a hand around just as he'd done a minute ago, "was what I was supposed to want. What I was supposed to pursue." I didn't like sharing this bit of myself with him, but I had to get him to understand. "I should get a man who would take care of me, someone who could provide this kind of life. That's what my mother did, and that's what she taught me to do." I felt small saying it. "I met Rick and thought he was the right guy."

He snorted. "From the first time I saw you two together, I could tell he wasn't right for you."

"Oh yeah?"

"Rick is fast and loose, looking for a woman around every corner. But you're not the kind of woman to be with someone like him, and I couldn't figure out why you *were* with him. What did you see in him? The money?"

I blushed with embarrassment that he so quickly saw Rick for who he was, and me for who I was, and that I'd been so dumb.

"Speaking of Rick," I chose my words carefully. "Do you know anything about him and Erin?"

"What about them?"

"That they … had an affair."

He stepped back as if I'd slapped him, then he blinked hard and shook his head. "No. I don't believe it. She wouldn't have done that."

"Caleb, Rick is saying they did."

His head kept shaking back and forth as he stared at the floor. "Erin and Rick. No way. Erin wasn't like that."

Erin wasn't like that, but Rick *was*. He was so sure of that. But did Caleb really know either of them? Did I?

I waited a minute, then said, "I know this is hard, but could something have been going on with Erin that you were missing? Had she been acting strangely? And what about that day? She went to the health club, but did she give you any hints about what she was going to do the rest of the afternoon?" The questions came out fast and harsh.

He hesitated as he looked up at me. "No."

I studied him. "What?"

"It's nothing."

"The night Erin was murdered, did you go out?"

He shook his head. "What? No."

"I heard your car."

"It wasn't mine. The only thing I did was call Tiffany to find out if she knew where Erin was, and she came over to talk."

"You told me that you'd called her and Melissa, but you didn't tell me that Tiffany had come over."

"I didn't?" He shrugged. "It was no big deal. She stopped by because she was worried, and we talked about where Erin might've gone. Neither of us had a clue."

"You never left your house?"

"No. I told you before, I stayed home the entire evening."

"Did something go on between you and Tiffany?" I whispered.

"No!" he said. "How could you think that?"

The truth was, I hated to ask it, but it had crossed my mind. And I found myself skeptical of his answer. But right then, I was suspicious and defensive about everything and everybody.

"Sometime during the night, headlights came down the street," I said. "Someone came home very late."

"It wasn't me." He frowned. "What is it with you staring out the window?"

"I don't know." I was even more defensive.

"At one point, it was kind of cute, but now I wonder about your obsession with me."

"That's fair." It was hard for me to admit that. "But at this point, I just want to find out what happened to Erin."

"So do I."

A long silence stretched out between us.

"Tiffany also told me about a fight you had with Erin," he finally said, "a few weeks before she died. Erin told you to stay away from me, and you said she should back off or else."

"That's not true," I said. "I didn't have a fight with Erin."

"So you don't deny saying what you did at the health club, but you deny the fight."

His tone said he didn't believe me. He took two steps toward me. I had never thought of Caleb as anything but sweet and kind, but right now his face was tense and unpleasant. I shifted my feet, but stood my ground.

"Were you and Erin having problems?" I asked gently.

He drew in a breath and it hissed out slowly. "Maybe things

weren't so great lately. I've been under a lot of stress, okay? And we were fighting over money. She was spending more than I was bringing in. But we still have … had a good marriage. And just because I was getting frustrated doesn't mean I killed her."

"Just like me saying that I'd kill for the life she had doesn't mean I'd do it," I said.

He tipped his head to the side, a subtle agreement, but he didn't smile.

"Did you tell the police what Tiffany said?" I asked.

"I haven't spoken to them since I talked to her, but she probably did."

I nodded. "Are the police still wondering about you?"

"I'm sure they are. I still have that life insurance policy on Erin."

"I'm so sorry."

"I don't know what's going on," he finally said. "I don't know what happened to my wife, but you shouldn't make up stories about what she was doing or who she was with. And you need to leave me alone."

"But Caleb, I've just been trying to help you," I protested.

"I've got enough help, okay? Please, just leave me alone."

I nodded mutely, and he turned around without another word and stalked out of the garage.

CHAPTER EIGHTEEN

My legs were wobbly as I stumbled into the house. I went immediately into the kitchen, filled a glass with tap water, and drank it down. It didn't help. My throat was parched. I wanted to throw up, and the walls seemed to close in on me.

I couldn't believe what Rick had told me was true. I'd known about his affair with Erin, but I'd been in such deep denial, I didn't believe it. I felt tears coming, and I pressed fists up to my eyes. I cried over my own stupidity, and then cried some more as Caleb came to mind. It hurt that he thought I might have had something to do with Erin's death.

I finally grabbed a Kleenex and blew my nose, then splashed water on my face. I took a kitchen towel and dried myself off, then sipped more water. My thoughts were jumbled and chaotic. In the past, when I'd had an especially hectic day at work – or when Rick and I'd had a fight – I'd go to the health club. A good workout had always centered me. I hadn't been to the club in forever. I stared out the back window at the tree branches swaying in a soft breeze, and decided "what the hell?" I might as well go work out now. I couldn't stay in the house right now. I went upstairs, found my gym bag, and packed workout clothes, shoes, and a brush and hairdryer, and then left.

***

The Cherry Hills Fitness Club was a health club located not too far from my house. It was expensive to be a member, and a lot of wealthy, well-connected, and locally famous people worked out there. It was where Erin and many others in my neighborhood went, so of course I'd felt I needed to go there as well. The membership fees were atrocious, and Rick had gotten mad when I'd told him I'd joined.

It was funny, I thought as I strolled through the front door. It really wasn't my kind of place. I enjoyed the workout, pushing my muscles, feeling the burn. I felt good after a visit, and I used to look forward to going there. For the women in my neighborhood, it was more about being seen and socializing.

I passed the front desk and headed toward the women's locker room, and as the faint smell of body odor hit me, I realized how much I missed being here. In the last several months, with everything that had gone on with Rick, I'd gotten out of the habit.

No more. I wouldn't let him ruin my life any longer.

I went into the locker room and changed clothes. Even though it had been a while, I recognized a few women. I gave them polite waves as I headed out into the weight room. I did a few sets on the machines with light weights, my muscles screaming the whole time. It had definitely been too long, and I was paying for it. I'd never been one to just glisten, and in no time I was sweating. I wiped my face with a towel and concentrated on my workout, not letting my mind mull over any-thing. Then I stopped and went into another room and hopped on a treadmill. I started a light jog, and that's when my thoughts turned to Rick.

Waves of disappointment washed over me. I'd married a schmuck, and then ignored what he'd done. Just like my mother. I'd known what he was doing, from that first woman to Erin. And who knows how many others. I'd denied it all. And now he was on to Sarah Papin. She appeared to have fallen for him. She was a lawyer, so she had to be smart – so how could she be so stupid to think Rick cared about her?

I snorted. I'd been stupid, too. I'd thought I could change Rick. Right. Sarah probably thought the same thing. Unless she hadn't figured out what he was really like. He was already showing his true colors if he was out with another woman the night Sarah and her husband had been at the dinner downtown, the night Erin had been murdered.

Who had Rick been with that night? He'd denied going to the Standard Motel, but it wouldn't surprise me if he had. Even though he had a place of his own, going to the Standard apparently gave him some kind of cheap thrill. If he'd taken Erin there, would she have gotten a thrill out of slumming there with him?

An image of her flashed in my mind. Erin, the perfect wife, the perfect partner for Caleb. And yet the brutal truth was that something had gone awry in their marriage, something that sent her looking elsewhere for companionship, sex, and maybe love. Things happened. Couples grew apart. I knew that. Hell, it had happened to me. But whatever had been going on behind the closed doors of the McCormick house, like the money trouble, must've gotten to her. And there had to be more to Caleb than I knew, even though, in my blind adoration, I couldn't see him being anything but doting and loyal. But something made Erin look elsewhere.

My thoughts grew dark. Not only had Erin cheated, but she'd cheated with *my* husband. I'd put her on a pedestal, even though she had been anything but kind to me. I'd thought her disdain had been because of how I felt about Caleb. But there was more to it. Had she gone after Rick because of what she'd perceived about Caleb and me? I could hardly believe she'd done that, but anything was possible. Or, it was possible Rick had decided to make her his latest conquest. He could have used his charms on her as he had done with so many other women, including me, and she wouldn't have been able to resist.

I slowed to a walk on the treadmill and shook my head in disgust. At Erin. At Rick. And at myself. As I began to look at things with a cold honesty, I had to look at Erin and Rick in a new light. What had she been up to before she'd been murdered? And had it led to her death? It was possible hers had been a random killing … or it could've been something more. My gut said it had to be the latter.

Suddenly things that I'd pushed into the shadowy corners of my mind began to play out like a movie. My looking out the window, Erin across the street, her hands on her hips as she glared at something – or someone. She hadn't been happy in that moment. Then her getting so angry with Rick the day she'd died. It kept coming back to that scene. Whatever they'd talked about, she'd not been happy with Rick.

Was he at the Standard that night? I should go back to the motel and ask around again. Then I asked myself whether that was a good idea. The police must have questioned everyone who'd worked there the night Erin was murdered. But that didn't mean I couldn't go and look for answers, I argued with myself.

I finally got off the treadmill. My legs were tired, but it was good tired. Getting rid of the tension tired, and I felt better than I had in a long while. I wiped off my face and walked back to the locker room. I stripped down, took a quick shower, and dressed. As I was packing up my gym bag, I noticed a familiar woman who was getting dressed for her workout. I knew her face, but couldn't remember her name. She'd been around when Erin, Tiffany, Melissa, and I had been here, before I'd decided to quit coming. She looked up, saw me, and gave me a short smile.

"I haven't seen you here in a while," she said, her voice soft.

"I've been kind of busy."

"Oh." She was tying her shoes, and she paused. "You live in the same neighborhood as Erin McCormick, right?"

"Yes," I said warily, not sure where she was going with this.

"You heard about her?"

I nodded.

"I was so surprised when I heard what happened to her." Her voice lowered, as if speaking of Erin might somehow be disrespectful.

"I was, too," I murmured.

"Did you know she was in here the day she died?"

My ears perked up. "Oh, really?"

"She'd come in to work out – you know." She blushed, realizing she was stating the obvious. "I can't believe that was the last time I saw her."

"What time was that?"

"It was about noon. I remember it was that day because I'd taken a shower and was toweling off and I heard her talking to someone else. Her voice was raised, like she was angry. It kind of surprised me, because usually Erin was pretty quiet when I saw her."

I leaned against a bank of lockers. "Who was she talking to?"

She shrugged. "I don't know. The other voice was muffled. I think the other woman was in the hall, and Erin's voice was echoing a bit, the way it does when you're near the locker room doors."

I nodded. "What did Erin say?"

She looked toward the ceiling, her hands still holding her shoestrings, and thought about it. "It was something about 'it's got to stop.' Then Erin said she would do exactly what she wanted, and she had a choice, too."

"I wonder what that was all about."

She looked down and finished tying her shoes. "Who knows?" Then she sat back and sighed. "I figured she was talking about a work-out."

"Did you see her at all after that?"

She shook her head. "No, she was gone by the time I came out to my locker."

"Nobody knows where she went after she left here."

"I'm afraid I don't, either. I just see her around here sometimes. I don't socialize with her outside of the health club." She stood up. "Do you know what the police have found out?"

"I don't." The last thing I was going to tell her was that the police seemed to think that I was somehow involved in Erin's death. Which was absurd.

"Well." She ran a hand through her hair. "I've got to get going. See you around."

"Right."

I followed her out the door, then turned and walked down the hall toward the front entrance. As I passed by the front desk, I saw a young woman typing at a computer. She'd worked here since I'd first started coming to the health club. I strolled over. She looked up and smiled.

"Hi, Mrs. Aldridge. How are you?"

"Pretty good," I said. "Do you have time for a quick question?"

"Sure."

"Were you working here on Sunday?"

The smile disappeared. "Erin McCormick died that night."

"You remember."

She nodded. "The police talked to me."

They had been here. No surprise. But what had they found out?

"I told them I remembered Erin coming in around ten-thirty, and she left around noon."

"She didn't act unusual?"

"Not at all. And," she held up a finger, "she wasn't with anybody. The police asked me that specifically. It was a day just like any other. Mrs. McCormick said hello as she passed by, and she left in a bit of a hurry because she didn't say anything when I told her to have a nice day."

"Was *that* unusual?"

She shrugged. "Not especially. It's just that some days I can tell she's in a hurry because she's a little curt. That was one of those days."

"And she wasn't with Tiffany Caruthers or Melissa Lowenstein?"

"Sure, they were around, but Mrs. McCormick didn't leave with them." She smiled. "I haven't seen you here in a while." She apparently didn't want to discuss Erin anymore.

"I'm out of practice," I said. "And I'll be paying for it now."

She laughed. "You have a good day."

"You, too."

I walked out the door and headed for my next stop.

CHAPTER NINETEEN

The Standard Motel was the same as always: cheap, rundown, and sleazy. There were no other words for it. I parked down the block from the motel. I didn't want anyone to think I had a reason to go there. Not that anyone I socialized with would be in this part of town, but you never knew. I got out and walked down the sidewalk toward the motel, and the desk clerk that I'd spoken to before was standing in the doorway, smoking a cigarette. He looked up, saw me, and his face pinched in recognition.

"Still don't know if that lady or your old man were here," he said, his voice scratchy.

I pursed my lips. "Oh, really?"

He took a drag on the cigarette. "Yep. Lots of people come and go. That's what I told the police."

"I see." I pulled out my phone. "Just for kicks and grins, have you ever seen this guy?"

I scrolled through photos until I found some of Caleb that I'd taken at a block party just after Rick and I'd moved into the neighborhood. I'd taken several pictures that day, but none of Rick and me. I found myself blushing now as I looked at the photo of Caleb. He was in profile, standing by himself, a beer in his hand, looking down the street. He'd been watching Erin as she talked with some of the other neighbors. I'd surreptitiously taken the photo, wanting one of Caleb without Erin, and had been pleased with how well it had turned out. I grimaced now. I really had been obsessed with Caleb. And I suppose I still was now. I'd deleted all my pictures of Rick, except the one, and I wasn't even sure why I'd kept that. But I had plenty of Caleb.

I swiped the screen until I found a good photo that showed Caleb's face, then held out my phone to the clerk. "Do you recognize this guy?"

He stared at the phone, then shook his head. "I don't recall seeing him at all. You think your ex was here with him?"

I quickly pulled the phone back. "No. I was wondering if he was here with the woman who was murdered."

"Oh." He shrugged. "I don't know."

"Did the police ask any of the other employees about Erin?"

"Who? Oh, the woman who died?" He nodded. "They did, but I don't know what all anybody told them. As far as I know, no one saw her around here. But again, lady, I told you, the people who work here don't want to say much, and the people who come and go don't want to be seen, if you know what I mean."

"Have you seen a woman with shoulder-length brown hair around lately?" I tried to describe Sarah Papin as best I could.

"Lady, that sounds like half the women in the world."

I laughed. "Yeah, it's not a very good description. I don't think I'd make a good detective, but I don't have a picture of her."

"Good luck with finding her."

I put my phone back in my purse, thanked him, and walked across the street to the Starbucks. It was crowded, lots of people stopping in after work. Pop music and the buzz of conversation permeated the coffee-scented air as I waited in line and ordered a latte, then found a table that looked out on Colfax. A woman with dyed black hair came over and wiped down some tables near me. When she finished, she glanced in my direction.

"Hey," I said.

She gave me an uninterested look. "Hi."

"Have you worked here for very long?"

She glanced around, seeming to wonder if she was in some kind of trouble. "About six months," she finally said.

"Do you recognize this woman?" I showed her the picture of Erin.

She glanced at the photo. "Yeah, she came in now and again."

"Any particular days?"

"Not really."

"She was killed not too long ago."

She glanced out the window and nodded. "Yeah, I know. I wondered why I hadn't seen her in here, and then the police came here asking questions."

"What did you say to them?"

She leaned against the wall near my table and her eyes grew distant. "The last time I saw that woman in here she was with a guy."

I pulled out my phone and quickly found the picture of Rick, then showed it to her. "Was it him?"

She took the phone from me and studied the photo for a moment. "Yeah, that's him." She handed the phone back. "I remember because she and that guy had a big fight."

"When was this?"

"The night she was murdered. They were here earlier that evening."

"What'd they fight about?"

"She had come in and bought a drink, and she went and sat over there." She gestured across the room. "He came in and went right over to her table and sat down. She acted surprised to see him and asked him to go away." She stared at the table where they'd sat. "They talked for a few minutes, and their voices got louder. Then she told him he was a bigger fool than she'd realized. He got mad and shouted, 'You can't do this to me,' and he slammed his hand down on the table. That got everyone's attention. I thought maybe we'd have to call the police because he looked so angry."

"What did Erin do? Was she scared?"

"The woman?" She shook her head. "Honestly, she looked as if she pitied him, like she was disgusted, you know? And she laughed at him, which just made him angrier. She finally told him to get lost, and then he begged her to listen to him. She just looked at him, and he finally got up and said, 'You'll get yours, you bitch.' And then he walked out. She just sat there, a smile on her face. She didn't seem to notice anyone around her. Then she finished her drink and left."

"Did you see where she went?"

"No, it was busy, and I had to get back to work."

"What time was this?"

"Around seven, maybe."

"Did you see her any more that evening?"

"No. We closed at eight, and I went home."

"And you've seen her here other times?"

"Oh, yeah, she pops in and out."

"Always with the same guy?"

"No, I've seen her with another guy, too."

I cocked an eyebrow. "What'd this other guy look like?" I swiped at my phone again and found the good picture of Caleb. "Him?"

She shook her head again. "Not him. Some other guy."

"Can you describe him?"

She looked past me and held up a hand. "I need to get back to work."

"What'd this guy look like?" I pressed.

"I don't know. A regular-looking guy." She shrugged. "Sorry."

"Did she ever fight with this other guy?"

"No, they seemed to be enjoying themselves. I don't know. Sorry, I've got to get back to work."

"What about a woman with shoulder-length brown hair? Was she ever in here with that guy, or the woman?"

She started to walk away. "I don't think so."

"Thanks," I said to her retreating back.

I sipped my latte, hardly tasting it as I looked out the window at the Standard Motel across the street. Rick had lied to me. He *had* been with Erin the night she'd been murdered. Probably at the motel, although I didn't have any definitive proof of that. The police might know, and if Rick had something to do with her death, they were probably closing in on him. But Erin had also been with another guy that night. Who was he, and had that man killed her?

I stood up and threw my half-drunk latte in the trash can, then headed out the door. I walked across the street, past the motel, and a-round the corner to the alley where Erin's body had been found. Dark shadows enveloped me as I walked down the alley to the dumpster. I looked past it, part of me thinking I'd see her lifeless body lying on the ground. But there was no trace that a murder had been committed here, just the foul odor from the dumpster, and the dirt and trash lying around. I wrinkled my nose. How had Erin ended up here?

A minute passed while I thought about her and that other man. Had she gone to the motel with him? Another affair that Caleb – and I – had denied? I wished I had a way to find out if she'd been a drug user, or if she had gotten mixed up with something illegal. I could call Kristen. Maybe her police contacts could shed some light on that.

I crossed my arms and continued on through the alley, emerging on the other side. There was a small shopping center and a large parking lot across the street. A few cars were scattered about. As I looked at the lot, a man in a business suit got out of a Honda Civic and crossed the street. He passed me, his head down, and went through the alley. I turned and watched him. He reached Colfax and turned left. I glanced back at his car. It looked as if he parked at the shopping center so no one would see him going to the motel. Or I could be making assumptions. I laughed to myself, then walked back through the alley.

As I stepped out onto the sidewalk, I stopped short. Detectives Maddow and Kowalski were standing in front of the motel. Maddow said something to Kowalski and then they disappeared into the motel. Five long minutes dragged by before they emerged. They hurried to their sedan and drove off. I shrank back into the shadows of the alley as the car passed by. Once it was gone, I dashed back to the motel and popped my head in the doorway. The clerk was behind the counter, a frown on his face.

"The police were just here," I said.

He nodded. "They were asking if you'd been here the night that woman was murdered. They had a picture of you." His eyes narrowed as he studied me closely. "You look prettier in person."

I gulped. "What'd you tell them?"

"The truth. I didn't see you here then."

"What about today?"

He shook his head, and he winked. "They didn't ask me about today."

I smiled. "I appreciate it."

"I know how to keep my mouth shut." Then he pointed at the street, where the detectives had just been. "I don't know what's going on between you and your husband and that woman, but I'd watch your back."

"I will."

I thanked him again and hurried back to my car.

CHAPTER TWENTY

It was now after five and Rick would be leaving work. I was certain he'd be meeting up with Sarah, although I doubted it would be at Benjamin's Bar, because I had a feeling their conversation wasn't going to be pleasant and they wouldn't want to have it in public. I drove downtown and parked in the lot near Union Station, then walked back toward his building. It was cloudy, with a hint of moisture in the air. I hoped it wouldn't rain. I stood in the doorway of a building across the street and waited.

Dusk faded to night, and I didn't worry that Rick or Sarah would see me. People walked up and down the block, going to restaurants in the area. I watched the windows of Rick's condo, my mind on him, and on this other man that Erin had seen the night she was murdered. Who was he? Her encounter with him could've been entirely innocent. But given that she had had at least one affair – with Rick – it was entirely possible she'd met this man for a dalliance that night. That still didn't mean that man had something to do with her death. Or did it?

My thoughts were in turmoil and I fidgeted, trying to stay quiet. I waited impatiently, and a little while later, a light went on in one of the windows in Rick's condo. Then he came out onto his deck. He leaned against the rail and peered into the darkness. I shrank back into the doorway.

Cars went by on the street, and then the sharp clack of heels on the sidewalk split the night air. Rick looked down the street, and so did I. Sarah Papin was walking purposefully toward his building. As she passed under a streetlight, I caught the look on her face. It was grim.

She was going to have it out with Rick. And once she'd finished, I was going to confront him as well. He'd lied to me about the night Erin had died. He'd most likely lied to the police, and to Sarah. Did she have any idea what he'd been up to? He may not tell her what he'd been up to, but he was going to tell me. One way or the other.

Sarah disappeared into his building, and a minute later, Rick turned around and went back into his condo. I waited and watched. Moments later, they emerged onto the deck. Sarah was animated, throwing her arms around. At one point Rick put his hands on her arms, and she jerked away. Snippets of their conversation drifted down to me.

"...believe you didn't tell me that..." she said.

A few people walking by glanced up toward them, but neither noticed. At one point, Rick raised his fist and she backed up. I held my breath, sure he was going to hit her. Then he appeared to calm down. They argued a bit longer, and he reached out to embrace her, but she put her hands on his chest and shoved him back. She stormed into the condo, with him at her heels.

For a brief moment, the night was eerily quiet. I held my breath until some cars drove by. Seconds later, the door to Rick's building flew open and Sarah burst outside. She shielded her face as she stalked down Wynkoop toward the Sixteenth Street Mall, her heels clacking like gunfire on the sidewalk. Had Rick hurt her? I hesitated. I wanted to talk to Rick, but I also wanted to see if Rick had hit her. I glanced at his condo.

He was standing in the balcony doorway, drinking. He'd be there a while. I quickly decided to follow Sarah.

I stayed on the other side of Wynkoop and kept her in sight. She made it to Sixteenth and went around the corner. I hurriedly crossed the street, not wanting to lose her. I was curious to see where she'd go. I rounded the corner and nearly slammed into her.

"What do you think you're doing following me?" she snapped, her hands on her hips.

"I ... uh ..." My mind was blank. I couldn't come up with any excuse so I resorted to staring at her.

The mall streetlights created shadows on her face. I could tell she'd been crying, but it didn't look like Rick had hit her. She wiped at her face and sniffed. I took a step back. The people who walked by seemed to disappear into the background as we talked.

"You were in love with him," I said.

It took a long time before she nodded.

She'd really fallen for Rick. How could she have been so stupid? And yet, I had been, too. Rick was slick, no doubt about it. When he wanted a woman, he reeled her in.

"Is that why you went to see him?" I asked. "To tell him how you felt?"

"When we met, he said you were out of the picture, that the divorce was almost final." She threw up a hand. "That was obviously a lie, and I wanted him to explain why you were so interested in us after all this time. He was furious that you'd confronted *me*. I told him it wasn't my fault, that you'd just shown up. How was I supposed to know that you were stalking us? Then I asked him if ..." A tear rolled down her cheek.

"You found out he doesn't love you."

She shook her head. "He's in love with somebody else."

My eyes narrowed. "Rick doesn't know how to love anybody."

Her face scrunched up as she tried to keep more tears from falling. "He'd said that he'd fallen for someone, that he'd never felt the things he was feeling for her."

"He told you that?" I asked, incredulous.

"Just now," she whispered.

I felt a stabbing pain in my chest. Rick, the man at one time I'd thought I'd loved – and thought he'd loved me – the man I thought I'd spend the rest of my life with – had found love with someone else. Could that actually be true? The someone else in question had to be Erin, but how could it have come to that?

"Did he tell you who it was?" I bit my lip, wanting – and not wanting – to hear the answer.

She shook her head again.

I thought for a second. "Why was he so angry with you?"

"You saw that?" Then she sighed. "Of course you did." She drew in a breath and let it out slowly. "He told me about that woman, and that he shouldn't have been seeing me at the same time he was seeing her. And he said he didn't mean to hurt me." She let out a bitter laugh. "Yeah, right. I got mad then, and asked him if there were other women besides her. He denied that, said it was just her and me, and that he was in love with her. At that point, I could barely see straight. I threatened to tell anybody and everybody about his affairs, including her husband. He wanted to know how I knew about them."

"How did you know?"

She snorted. "I don't know who the woman is, let alone her

husband. I just know it was a neighbor where he used to live."

"He told you that?"

"Yes. I said I'd knock on all the doors in the neighborhood and tell everyone about him. That's when he raised his hand and said he'd stop me if he had to, that I wasn't to tell anyone about her."

"Erin."

"That's the woman you were asking about? The one who'd been murdered?"

I nodded. "He was with her that night."

"No." She was adamant. "I asked him if he was with her then, and he denied it."

But he was with Erin, I thought. I was puzzled about why Rick would lie about that.

"They were seen together at a coffee shop near where her body was discovered," I said.

She sighed heavily. "He denied sleeping with her that night."

A mall shuttle bus passed by and we both stared at it. People got on and off, and I wished I was one of them, someone who didn't have the troubles I did. I glanced at Sarah. Was she thinking the same thing?

"What're you going to do now?" I asked, my voice heavy in a sudden stillness.

"I don't know," she murmured.

"Do you still love your husband?"

She looked away, her face pained. "I don't know. I still like him. He's my friend. But ..."

"You can make it right with him, if you want."

She turned back to me. "I don't know what was going on with you and Rick and that woman, but leave me alone, okay? And stay away from my husband."

With that, she spun around and walked down the mall. I watched until she vanished into the night, and then I turned and walked back towards Rick's building.

CHAPTER TWENTY-ONE

A streak of lightning momentarily lit up the dark sky as I walked back up Wynkoop to Rick's condo. I opened the door I'd seen Sarah emerge from, and stepped into a lobby with a bench. Next to an interior glass door was a bank of buttons, each one labeled with a unit number. I didn't want Rick to know I was paying him a visit, so I waited until I heard the sound of voices on the other side of the glass. Then I moved over to the door and pretended that I was about to use a key. A man and a woman came out, and the man held the door for me. I thanked him and hurried inside.

I walked down a short hall and went left. Across from an elevator were mailboxes. I looked and found one with a label that read "Aldridge." Rick's condo. I probably could've figured out which unit was his, but no sense in taking chances. I didn't want to bang on doors until I found the correct one.

I rode an old elevator up to the third floor and walked down a hallway with dark carpet that muffled my footsteps. When I got to Rick's door, I hesitated, then drew in a breath and knocked. A few long seconds passed, then the door swung open.

"I'm so glad you came ba–" he said, then stopped when he saw me. "Get lost."

He'd obviously thought Sarah would return. He started to shut the door, but I put out my hand to stop it.

"Don't, Rick," I said. "I need to talk to you."

"Go away."

My hand didn't waver. "I'm not leaving until I know what's going on with you."

"You think you're a detective, huh? You think you've figured it all out."

"I still don't know who killed Erin."

"It wasn't me," he said in a low voice.

I glanced around, not at all sure what I believed. "Let me in so we can talk."

He could've pushed the door shut on me, but didn't. He gazed at me, his eyes cold. A small glass in his hand held a finger's worth of some brown liquid. He took a slug and drained it, then blew out an alcohol-laced breath that almost knocked me over. He wagged his head in resignation, backed away from the door, and turned around.

"Come on in," he called over his shoulder.

I stepped inside and shut the door, then followed him down a wide hallway with dark hardwood floors. We turned a corner and passed an open doorway to a bedroom. A large unmade bed filled the space. A few shirts were tossed on the floor. Same old Rick. Past that, we emerged into an open living area. The place had an industrial feel, with exposed ceilings and brick walls. Rick hadn't done much in terms of decorating, just a couch and loveseat, a TV, and a few small pictures on the walls.

He walked over to the kitchen on the other side of the room, plunked his glass on the counter, and grabbed a bottle of Crown Royal. He raised it up and looked at me.

"You want a drink?"

I shook my head. "No, thanks."

"Oh yeah. You don't drink much. That hasn't changed since I left?" The sarcasm was clear.

I shook my head again.

He filled his glass, swirled the ice around, and took a long drink. I could tell from knowing him as long as I had that he was a little drunk. But he held his liquor well. He leaned against the counter and stared at me.

"Man, I can't believe what you've done."

I perched on the edge of the couch and put my hands in my lap. "You're the one that's screwed things up, not me. Part of the problem is you've never been honest with anyone, including yourself."

He stared at me. "You're going to psychoanalyze me now?" When I didn't reply, he said, "What does that mean?"

"You're a player. You always have been. You always will be. And now you've dragged Sarah into this."

He scratched his forehead. "It's not what you think."

"Enlighten me. What's going on? You want me to believe you're not banging Sarah?"

He snorted. "Of course I am – was. I've known her for a while." He quickly held up a hand. "Before you ask, no, I wasn't seeing her when we were married."

"We still *are* married."

He sneered. "We've been over this. Anyway, I liked her, but nothing happened until I moved out."

"How'd you meet her?"

"I met her at my lawyer's office. I saw her a few times and asked her out."

"And you were also seeing Erin."

"On and off. I started seeing Sarah in an off time."

I asked the question even though I knew the answer would be painful. "You were seeing Erin for longer than a few months, right?"

"It started last summer. Like I said, it wasn't anything steady."

I swallowed hard. "That long?"

He shrugged.

"Why didn't it continue?"

He looked past me, out the glass door that opened onto his deck.

"Erin was seeing someone else," he said.

"Who?" I asked in a soft voice.

"I don't know. It had been going on for a while before she was murdered."

I studied him closely, surprised by the bitter tone in his voice. "You were jealous of that other man, weren't you?"

He glanced away, then nodded slowly. I scrutinized him even more. His eyes fell, and then he hung his head.

"Oh my god," I said, stunned. "You thought you were really in love with Erin."

He rubbed a hand over his jaw. "You don't know what she was really like."

Maybe not in bed, I thought. But I'd been privy to her callousness, and it wouldn't have made me want to love her.

"It sounds like she was a player, too." I hoped the comment would hurt.

He grimaced. "No, you don't understand. There was something about her. When we were together … I can't describe it."

I couldn't believe what I was hearing. "Wait a minute. You're the party animal, the guy who can't keep his dick in his pants, all of that. You *really* thought you had something with Erin?"

He finally made eye contact with me. "It sounds crazy."

"Yes, it does."

"I don't know how to explain it."

"Did Caleb ever suspect anything?"

"He was too caught up in his work, and thinking she was so perfect. I told you, he adored her, and she hated it." He laughed. "He thought everything was okay, but she was getting sick of how old and stale their life was. He never saw that she had a wild side."

He took another drink and gave me a look as if daring me to challenge him. Erin with a wild side? I decided to let that part go.

"You and Erin," I murmured. I'd never be able to explain to myself how he could've fallen for Erin. "You saw her the night she died." He started to protest, but I interrupted. "Don't. You were at the Starbucks across the street from the motel. They recognized your picture and remembered you meeting Erin there."

"Man, you have been busy."

"The police and other people think I might've had something to do with Erin's death, so I'm going to get to the bottom of this."

He took a long time before saying something. "Fine. I met her there."

"She wasn't expecting you. That's what one of the women who works there told me."

He set his glass down. "Erin was meeting someone else there, and yeah, she was surprised to see me."

"You told her you didn't want her to see the other guy." I took his silence as acknowledgement. "And what? You asked her to leave Caleb and be with you?"

"No."

That was a lie.

"You wanted her to."

He frowned. The rejection had hurt him badly. I never thought I'd see that in him.

"You're the man who could have any woman you wanted. But not her. Maybe that's why she was so attractive to you."

His shoulders went up slightly, then drooped down. Something occurred to me.

"Was that what you two were talking about that afternoon when I saw you outside our house?"

He nodded slowly. "She didn't want to see me anymore, and I told her I wouldn't accept that. She got angry and told me she'd moved on, and I should too."

Move on. Those were familiar words – words he'd been saying to me – but I don't think he heard the irony in it.

"The way she said it," he went on, "I knew she would be seeing that guy that night. But I couldn't let it go, so I went to the Starbucks because I knew that's where she'd be. She'd get a cup of coffee, make sure no one had followed her, and then she'd go over to the motel. Or sometimes we'd meet for coffee first before heading to our room."

"Did you see the man she was meeting?" I asked.

He shook his head.

"You really thought you could talk her out of seeing him?"

He bit his lip but remained silent.

"Wow, you really had fallen for her," I said.

"I never expected it to happen."

"The woman I talked to said you left the coffee shop first, and Erin left a while later."

"Yeah."

"Did you see who she met?" I repeated.

"It might've been a guy who drove a dark car. But I thought Erin noticed me, and I didn't want her to know I'd been spying on her, so I took off before I saw who the guy was."

"The clerk at the motel doesn't remember you, but how do I know you didn't meet her at the motel, that this whole story of the other guy is a lie?"

"I'm telling the truth," he snapped. "She met another guy."

I raised my hands defensively. "Or you waited until Erin finished whatever she was doing with this other man, and then you killed her because you were jealous."

He came around the counter and strode up to me. I held my ground and he stared down at me. His eyes were wide with anger. I felt my nerves tingle and I braced myself.

"You don't have any way of knowing that, and neither do the police, because I don't have an alibi. After I saw Erin, I came home and spent the rest of the night here, alone. That's the way it was." His nostrils flared. "Now, on top of everything else, things are screwed up with Sarah. And Erin's dead. There's nothing you can do about any of it, but I want you to leave me alone. It's over between us. Sign the papers I left at your house and we'll be out of each other's hair forever. Okay?"

I thought about the headlights I'd seen that night. I screwed up my courage and went on. "Have you been in the neighborhood, parked down the street, watching our house?"

"No." The word was filled with venom.

I couldn't tell if that was the truth or not.

"I told you, I came home that evening and stayed here. And I haven't been in the neighborhood except the two times you've seen me."

"I'm not asking just about *that* night."

He glanced away.

"Rick."

"All right. I parked down the street sometimes. I wanted to know if she was out late… with him."

"Quit dodging the question. Were you parked there *that* night?"

He shook his head.

I shifted away from him, and he stood with his legs apart and stared at me.

"I'll go now," I said.

"I think that's wise. Let's be done with each other, okay?"

As I looked at him, I felt a little sorry for him. He was hurting, not because of the demise of our marriage, but because he actually knew what it felt like to love someone and not have them love you back. It stung. But I also wondered if that had driven him to murder Erin.

I suddenly felt the need to get out of there. I whirled around and hurried down the hall and out his front door. I couldn't get out of the building fast enough, and it wasn't until I was walking down Wynkoop that I breathed again.

CHAPTER TWENTY-TWO

I gripped the steering wheel hard as I drove home, my eyes focused straight ahead into the dark night. Rick had confirmed a lot of things, but no matter how much I thought about it, I didn't have any idea who Erin's other lover had been. I was still having a hard time believing this new information about her. But then, I was the only one who'd thought she was perfect.

Whoever Erin had been mixed up with had to be involved somehow with her death. It didn't make sense otherwise that her body had been found so close to the motel where she'd been having multiple affairs. Erin, it seemed, had been more of a player than Rick. Maybe she'd rejected another lover just as she had Rick. Maybe that's who'd killed her.

I flipped back to Rick. He wasn't the type to take rejection lightly. He was so sure of himself, so sure of everything he did, and he prided himself on his ability to woo women. And he was angry. I'd seen him angry with Erin and Sarah. And even with me just before I'd left him tonight. I bit my lip. He was certainly capable of killing Erin.

I thumped the steering wheel, not sure what to believe.

It was past ten when I drove into my neighborhood and down the quiet street to my house. I hit the garage door opener and pulled my car into the garage. I went into the kitchen and it hit me then that I was famished. There was hardly any food in the house, so I fixed a sandwich and ate it slowly while standing at the kitchen counter. I looked out into the dark back yard, thinking about all of the plants that needed tending to. And yet I hadn't done a thing, and now my focus was elsewhere. It's funny how the things that once gave you joy can suddenly lose their charm and become a chore. That's what the yard felt like right now.

A memory crept into my consciousness, a time when I'd been out front planting flowers in a bed near the garage. Erin had walked by while I'd been working. This was after she'd picked up on my obsession with Caleb. She gave me an icy glare that also held a hint of disdain, as if pitying me for having to do my own gardening.

I should've realized at the time the difference between her and me. She couldn't recognize that gardening was something I enjoyed, that it gave me a sense of peace and centeredness, almost like my workouts at the health club. For her, her sense of purpose had come from something else. At the time I hadn't thought much about it, other than to think she didn't need to be cool to me, but now I saw more meaning in that memory. Given what I'd found out, perhaps Erin had been searching for something herself, trying to find it by chasing men or putting herself in dangerous situations. Had she pushed it too far, and had it cost her her life?

My sandwich was gone, and I finally dragged myself upstairs. I took a quick shower and crawled into bed, but I lay for a long time in the dark, staring up at the ceiling. That seemed to be a lot of what I was doing lately.

I closed my eyes, and an image of Rick came to mind. He's standing with something in his hand, a rock or board. Erin is there, and they are arguing. She is laughing at him, mocking his feelings toward her, telling him that she doesn't want him, that he is stupid to fall for her. He raises his hand again as he strikes her in the head, knocking her out. He hits her again, this time with lethal force. Then he's carrying her body from a sleazy motel room to the alley nearby, heaving her lifeless form near the dumpster.

I scrunched my eyes up, trying to rid myself of the vision, and yet it wouldn't go away. I lay for a long time, my breath coming in short gasps, the sheets wet with sweat. Then a car came down the street, and the particular vibration of the engine was familiar. Headlight beams crossed the ceiling. I pushed myself out of bed, went to the window, and peered out. Caleb's black Mercedes drove by. It pulled into his driveway and disappeared into his garage. I glanced at the clock. It was after midnight.

What was he doing out so late?

I watched his house, the image of Rick gone. Something nudged at me, a thought I kept trying to push away. Was it possible that Caleb was the killer? He had plenty of reasons to be upset with his wife. He could've found out about her and Rick. He could have lied to me about that, knowing I would believe him.

A light went on in an upstairs window of Caleb's house. Time ticked by, and after a while, the light went out. The house remained dark. I stared into the night for a long time, not tired at all now. I finally went downstairs, logged onto the computer, and got on the Internet.

I searched on Caleb McCormick again and tried to find more about him, but couldn't. He was an enigma to the world, as he was to me. I knew nothing about this man that I'd lusted after, just as he'd known nothing about his wife.

What if there was more to Caleb than I wanted to admit? He was having money troubles, and he said that he and Erin had been fighting. What if he knew about Erin's affairs and was having some of his own? Tiffany appeared tight with him. She'd gone over to his house the night Erin had been murdered. It was possible that he and Tiffany were involved. I'd been avoiding Tiffany, but I should probably talk to her, too.

I ended up on Erin's Facebook page, reading her posts. So many pictures of her. I studied her face closely. I began to see something behind her smiles, a suggestion that she hadn't been as happy as she'd acted.

I finally shook my head, turned off the computer, and went back upstairs. I still lay awake for a long while, wishing the time would go by and all this would be resolved. Somewhere along the way, I fell asleep.

***

The next morning, Friday, I got up early, feeling sluggish, as if I'd drunk too much. I had a cup of coffee while I stood looking out the living room window. The street was still, but my thoughts were not. I needed to talk to Caleb, but my will was weak. He might slam the door in my face. I didn't know if I could face that rejection right now.

I shook my head, trying to clear my mind. As I took the last sip of coffee, I saw Melissa come out of her house and head next door to Tiffany's. She rang the bell, and when Tiffany came out, they stood on the front porch talking. Then I did something I hadn't had the courage to do in years. I set my cup down, but instead of meekly going into the kitchen, I marched out the door, down the driveway, and across the street. It was a gorgeous spring day, pleasantly warm and dry. Both women glared at me as I approached.

"What do you want?" Tiffany asked.

My gaze darted between them. Tiffany was irritated that I'd interrupted, but Melissa seemed more put-off than upset.

"I don't know what's going on, or what you've been telling Caleb," I said. "But I didn't have anything to do with Erin's death."

Both crossed their arms, almost like twins.

"Amber," Melissa said. "I don't know what all went on between you and Erin, but I know she wasn't happy with you at all. But at this point, we don't know what to think about who murdered her."

My voice nearly cracked. "You can't possibly believe I would kill her."

She shrugged. "To be honest, no, but I've never been in this kind of situation, and I don't know what to believe. But I do know you two didn't like each other, and I know you were jealous of her, of what she had, and the fact that she was married to Caleb. You're going through a difficult divorce. I know things are tough, but ..." Her voice trailed off.

"None of that means anything," I said.

"People have killed for a lot less." There was venom in Tiffany's voice.

"And you had that fight with Erin before she died," Melissa said.

I was exasperated. "What fight?"

"The one where she told you to stay away from Caleb," she replied.

"You didn't hear me," I protested, "because it didn't happen."

They both looked at me, eyebrows raised. They didn't believe me.

"I suppose you both told the police all this," I said.

Neither looked me in the eye, and I knew that was exactly the case.

"When is the funeral?" I asked.

"You're not going," Tiffany said.

"What?" I stepped back. "You can't stop me."

"I don't know if that's a good idea," Melissa said.

I shook my head. "I did *not* murder Erin."

"The funeral is about Caleb," Tiffany said. "And your being there isn't a good idea."

They both stood and stared past me uncomfortably.

"Fine," I finally snapped. "I'll go ask Caleb."

"Don't go over there," Tiffany said.

"Try and stop me," I replied.

Melissa was the voice of reason. "I don't know if it's a good idea for you to go to the funeral, given what the police think." I opened my mouth, but she held up a hand. "I'm not trying to be mean, and let's assume you didn't have anything to do with her death–"

"I didn't," I interrupted harshly.

"Okay," she went on, "but I don't know if Caleb wants to see you."

"There's something important I need to discuss with him," I said.

I turned around and walked defiantly down the sidewalk. I could feel their eyes bore into my back, but I wasn't going to let them bully me. As I strode up Caleb's sidewalk, I glanced over at them. Both of them had it in for me. I was still shocked that they could really believe I might've murdered Erin. It made me even more certain that I had to find Erin's killer, and fast.

CHAPTER TWENTY-THREE

I reached Caleb's front porch, and my courage suddenly waned. I squared my shoulders and pressed the doorbell. I didn't care what Tiffany or Melissa thought, I was going to find out what I could about Erin's death, and that meant I had to speak to Caleb. Tiffany, Melissa, and anyone else in the neighborhood who suspected me needed to know the truth. I waited, my heart thumping. The door swung open and Caleb stared at me for a moment.

"I don't want to talk to you," he said.

"Please, Caleb, it's important." He started to close the door, and I went on. "I found out more about Erin. Please, you've got to help me!"

The door stopped, and then he opened it wider. He still didn't act as if he wanted to let me in, but he finally stepped aside and I moved into the foyer. There was no hint of cologne as at other times I'd seen him. I heard voices in another room.

"My mother-in-law and sister-in-law are here," he said. "We're working on funeral arrangements."

"I see," I murmured.

Just then, a woman with short gray hair poked her head into the hallway.

"Is everything okay?" she asked.

Caleb held up a hand. "I'll just be a minute, Myrna."

The woman looked at me, her eyes wide with curiosity, and then she disappeared. In that brief moment, I saw Erin in her face.

"Your mother-in-law?" I whispered to Caleb.

He nodded.

"When is the funeral?"

He hesitated. "It'll be next Tuesday."

"I'd really like to come."

"I don't know if that's a good idea."

"Caleb, I know Melissa and Tiffany—"

"Come in here," he interrupted as he glanced down the hall to where Myrna had been.

He led me into an office with a large mahogany desk and matching bookcases. He went around the desk and sat down at a big leather chair. He waited and I took a seat on a wingback chair across from him.

"I know Melissa and Tiffany are telling you things about me, but none of it's true."

He didn't say anything to that, and I took a moment to survey him. He didn't look like the fine piece of a man that I'd had the hots for. He appeared tired and stressed – and why wouldn't he be? Dark circles ringed his eyes, and he hadn't shaved in a few days. But the stubble of beard didn't make him look sexy anymore; he just looked haunted. He seemed thinner, too. His cheeks were sunken in, as if he'd lost several pounds in just the last few days.

"Is that all you want to tell me?" he asked.

I shook my head and swallowed a lump in my throat. "I know this is hard for you to hear, but I talked to Rick last night. He was definitely having an affair with Erin."

He didn't say a word, just stared at me for the longest time. Then his eyes slowly moved to the front window and he gazed out into the front yard. He drew in a breath and let it out slowly, then steepled his hands.

"Okay."

If I expected more, I didn't get it. I was surprised.

"Don't you believe me?" I asked.

He continued to look out the window, and his eyes finally swung toward me. "I guess. I don't know what to believe anymore."

"Have you learned anything more about her?"

"Obviously when your wife is having an affair, and she's discovered in an alley near a motel, and you have no idea why she was there, maybe there was more to her than you realized. I think about the times where she wasn't coming home, and ..." He stopped for a second, then cleared his throat. "Obviously she was doing something with ... Rick ... and I just didn't want to see it."

"I hate to tell you this, but there was someone else besides Rick."

He looked at me, his eyes hollow. "Who?"

"That's the thing. I don't know who it was, but the night she was murdered, she'd gone to a Starbucks near the motel. Rick said he met her there and they talked for a while, but then he left."

"So? She was just having coffee."

"Rick thinks she was meeting someone else at the motel later."

"He doesn't know who it was?"

I shook my head. "No."

A calculated gleam came into his eyes. "Do you believe him?"

I pursed my lips. "To be honest with you, I don't know. Rick has a mean streak, and I've seen it in him the last few times I've talked to him.

And he admitted to me that he was in love with Erin. So …"

He unsteepled his hands and laid them on the desk. "He was in love with her?"

"Yes."

It took him a long time to answer. "I don't know what to say to that."

"I think he'd fallen for her in a big way."

He nodded. "When Erin wanted to, she could be incredibly charming."

"Rick said the same thing," I murmured. I didn't want to say that I'd never seen the charming side of Erin. "Regardless, Erin told Rick she wasn't interested in him in any romantic way, and he didn't like hearing that. He was jealous and rejected."

He leaned back. "Enough to murder her?"

I shrugged. "That's the question."

"She wasn't interested," he said softly, "and it wasn't because she cared about me."

The pain in his voice hurt me.

"I hate to do this," I said, "but let's think about it all for a minute. When someone has an affair, there might be signs. Did Erin get any phone calls at odd times?"

"No, and no texts, either. I trusted her, so I didn't look at her phone or her email."

"Have you done any of that since her death? Did you find anything?"

He shook his head. "Nothing."

"Are you sure?"

"Yes."

"Did she act funny with anyone in the neighborhood?"

"Besides you?"

I gulped. "Uh, yes."

"No."

"What about Rick?"

"Neither one of us caught what was going on between them."

"Well ..."

He arched an eyebrow. "You knew."

I shook my head. "I suspected it, but Rick denied it."

"And you didn't want to face the truth."

I shrugged.

"I know," he said. "Kind of like me."

"But you didn't suspect anything at all?"

"No."

His answers were so flat, I couldn't tell whether he was chiding himself for his naiveté or he just didn't want to tell me he'd found something.

He rubbed his jaw. "Come on, let's face it. I was the gullible husband, and she pulled the wool over my eyes while she obviously," he waved a hand in the air, "was doing all kinds of things that I knew nothing about."

"Do you think she was on drugs or anything like that?"

"No. I know, how would I know?" The hand came up again. "But she didn't act that way. If she was doing drugs, I would've seen signs, something in her behavior, but there was nothing. I admit, we liked our wine and cocktails, and she had the occasional extra drink or two, and we sometimes got drunk. But that was it. The police asked those questions, and they're looking into it all, too. I don't know what they'll find, but it won't be drugs."

I couldn't think of what else to ask, and an uncomfortable silence ensued. He finally broke it.

"Do you know what it's like to wake up one day and suddenly your wife's gone, and everything you thought you had with her was an illusion, that she didn't care about you at all?"

"No, but I know what it's like to have the person you thought you loved not love you back."

He frowned. "Yeah, I guess you do. I keep thinking about all the things I should've done differently. I should've changed."

"Would it have made any difference?"

He didn't answer.

As I stared at him, I couldn't bring myself to believe he had anything to do with Erin's death. And yet, that thought still tickled at the back of my mind. Something else occurred to me.

"Where were you last night?" I asked.

He snickered. "You're always looking out the window, huh? You noticed I came home late."

I let out a small, nervous laugh. "I'm sorry. I couldn't sleep, and I heard your car."

"I was out with some guys from work. And yes, in case you want to check up on me, I can prove it."

I felt bad for asking the question. "No, that's okay."

"But I still don't have an alibi for the night Erin died."

We contemplated each other for a minute. His face didn't betray anything of what he was thinking of me. I was thinking about how, if he had murdered Erin, he was doing a great job of the bereaved husband. He couldn't have done it, I repeated to myself, over and over.

"I know you mean well," he finally said. "And I shouldn't have thought you had anything to do with Erin's death, but right now I really do need my space." But suspicion filled his eyes.

"You can't believe what Melissa and Tiffany told you. They're wrong."

"Right now I don't know what to believe. But I don't think you should come to the funeral. Not because of me, but because of them. I don't need a scene there."

"I'd just like to pay my respects."

He threw me a wan smile. "You didn't like Erin anyway."

I started to protest, but he interrupted. "Consider your respects paid, and I appreciate it."

I heard a feminine voice, a clearing of the throat. Caleb glanced up, and I turned around. His mother-in-law was walking back down the hall. Caleb stood up.

"If you'll excuse me, I do have a lot to do. Whatever you find about Erin, I don't want to know. Not right now."

I got up. "Sure."

He led me to the door and opened it. "Take care of yourself."

"You do the same." I stepped outside and the door quietly closed behind me.

CHAPTER TWENTY-FOUR

I walked slowly back across the street. Melissa and Tiffany weren't outside anymore, but I still felt like their eyes were on me. I glanced at both of their houses, but I didn't see either one in their windows. It was probably my imagination.

I went inside my house and called Kristen. She was in a meeting, so I left a message for her to call me as soon as she could. I wanted to find out whether she'd heard anything more from her police connections about Erin's murder, or what they had found about Caleb. I also wanted to know what the police knew about Rick.

I was antsy, my nerves on edge after my talk with Caleb and my encounter with Melissa and Tiffany. I stared at the phone, willing Kristen to return my call. The phone didn't ring. I finally took my coffee cup into the kitchen and rinsed it out. My hands shook as I loaded it in the dishwasher. I needed to clear my mind, to let things go. I took a deep breath as I looked out the window. The yard was a mess, dead leaves in the flower beds, bushes that needed to be cut back, flowers that needed to be planted. I couldn't do it all at once, but I decided right then that I could at least start on things while I waited for Kristen to call me back.

Decision made, I went out back and into the shed. I grabbed a metal rake and began raking the dead leaves and weeds out of the flower beds along the fence between my yard and Kayla's. It was hard work, but it felt good, the sun warm on my skin. I soon had a big pile, so I stopped and leaned my rake against the shed, then filled a trash bag with the dead leaves. As I tied up a bag, I heard something on the other side of the fence.

"Is that you, Amber?" It was Kayla.

I paused and wiped sweat from my brow. "Yeah. How are things?"

"Not too bad," she said.

I peered through a large crack in the fence and saw her. "Can I ask you a question?"

"Sure."

I hurried to the gate and went over into her yard, then opened her gate. "Was Tiffany ever interested in Caleb?"

She laughed. "Are you kidding? Caleb and Erin have a great marriage. And so do John and Tiffany."

"I see." She obviously was in the dark about Erin's affairs.

"Tiffany and Erin are – were – best friends. Other than that one fight, they've been best pals."

"What fight?"

She sighed. "It was a few weeks back. Since they live right next door to each other, they're always talking over their fence, or in their driveways, or one's popping over to visit the other. So I see them outside a lot. Anyway, there was one day when I was coming home from the grocery store, and it looked like they were fighting. Well, let me back up. Tiffany didn't look very happy, and Erin was kind of jabbing her finger at Tiffany. Then Tiffany spun around and ran back in her house."

"Did you hear any of the conversation?"

"No. And it must've been nothing because the next time I saw them together, a few days later, everything seemed to be fine. I'm sure it was nothing, and I'm making more of it than it was."

"I guess so," I said.

She wagged a finger in the air. "Now Erin and Melissa – they could sometimes have spats. But you know how it is among friends." She glanced over her shoulder. "I need to get back inside. Talon will be waking up soon. It's good to see you outside. I know how much you like your garden and flowers."

"Thanks."

She left, but I wasn't in a yardwork mood anymore, so I went back through my back yard. I carried the full leaf bag to the garage, then went into the house. I checked my phone again, but Kristen still hadn't called. I fixed a salad with lettuce that was probably on the edge of spoiled, and reminded myself I needed to get to the grocery store. I stood at the window, waiting for Kristen to call back. Time crept by, and the walls began to close in on me.

I thought maybe a trip to the health club would help, so I put workout clothes in a gym bag and drove there. I didn't see anyone I knew, but it felt good to be pushing my muscles and breathing hard. For a brief time, my problems vanished. Between that and working in my garden again, I could resume some sense of normality. Normal as much as it could be, given everything that was going on.

I finished my workout, showered, and changed clothes, and Kristen still hadn't called. I left the health club, but I didn't want to go home, so I drove around. I passed by a restaurant that I knew Erin and Caleb liked. I parked in the lot and watched the front door for a while, not at all sure what I was doing, then left and eventually found myself parked near the Standard Motel. I sat for a while, picturing Erin there with Rick. Images of a new, faceless man, appeared in my vision. I was about to leave when my phone rang.

"There you are," I said to Kristen.

"I'm so sorry, I've been tied up in court," she said breathlessly. "You're staying out of trouble, right?"

"Yeah. Hey, have you heard anything more from your police contacts about Erin's murder?"

"Why? What have you found out?"

I told her everything I'd learned in the last few days, including what Rick had told me last night.

"So you aren't staying out of trouble," she said when I finished.

"I can't let this go."

"Maybe, maybe not." She growled. "Do you think Rick is lying?"

"I don't know. He was livid about my talking to Sarah."

"I can see that."

"And the police thinking I'm a suspect, it's silly."

"It is, but you need to back off."

"I can't."

She let out a big sigh. "Tell you what, let me make a phone call or two, then I'll swing by the house. I need to get out of here for a bit."

"I'm not at home. Meet me at Starbucks."

"Which one?"

I gave her the address.

"Nice part of town," she said sarcastically. "Why are you there? Wait, that's where Rick was, at the motel."

I didn't say anything.

"Okay," she finally said. "I'll be there in half an hour or so."

I hung up and walked across the street to the coffee shop. I ordered a macchiato and sat down at a corner table, where I could look outside. I stared at the motel. All the people that went in and out of there, the clandestine affairs, the hookups with prostitutes. How many lives were ruined, including mine? I should've left Rick a long time ago, when I knew he'd been seeing someone else, but I hadn't. Would I be involved in all this if I had left him then? I was still mulling that over when Kristen walked in. She strode over to my table, bent down, and gave me a quick hug.

"How're you doing?"

"Not too bad," I said.

"Let me get something to drink."

She went to the counter and returned with a tall latte. She sat down, and the air around us filled with tension.

"Man, it's been a helluva day," she said as she sipped her drink.

"I know. You normally call me back right away."

"I'm sorry."

I studied her. She blinked several times. "What?" I asked.

"I talked to my friend in the police department. You're still a suspect."

"That's ludicrous."

"Maybe, but they don't think they can eliminate you just yet. You had fights with Erin, you threatened her, and you don't have an alibi for the night she was murdered."

I shook my head. "Unbelievable."

She held up a hand. "They also still suspect Rick and Caleb."

"I don't think Caleb did it."

She cocked an eyebrow at me. "You're still talking to him?"

"This morning," I said a little sheepishly.

"Huh. I wonder what the police will think about that."

"If they find out I did," I said. What if Melissa or Tiffany told them? I left that unsaid.

"And your take on Caleb is he's innocent."

"Yes, or he's a really good actor. He's also incredibly naïve because he didn't seem to have any idea Erin was cheating on him at all."

"He's still a solid suspect, mostly because of the insurance policy."

"Did they find anything? What about phone records or emails, things like that?"

Her fingers drummed the table. "Nothing that would either incriminate Caleb or clear him. But I don't know much more than that. Whatever she was doing, it's not recorded anywhere."

"Did Caleb erase anything?"

"I don't know about that." She tipped her head. "Did you get some sun today?"

"I did some yardwork while I was waiting for you to call back."

"Good. You need to get back into your routines instead of just staring out the window and worrying about all this."

I nodded. "I guess you're right."

She sipped her drink and glanced outside. "If this man that Erin met the night she was murdered wasn't Rick, and it wasn't Caleb, who was it?"

"That's the million-dollar question. It could've been someone she knew from the club, or who knows."

"What about someone else in the neighborhood?"

I shrugged. "My next-door-neighbor Kayla and her husband seem to have a good relationship, and they both dote on their baby."

"Maybe she's tired and he's looking somewhere else for sex."

I laughed. "I suppose so, but I doubt it. And Melissa and Tiffany both have good marriages."

"Well, I don't know then."

"Yeah, but until the police eliminate me as a suspect, I'm going to keep at it."

"Be careful asking around." She gulped down the last of her latte. "I hate to tell you this, but I've got another meeting."

"It's okay."

"You be careful. And sign that paperwork so we can get Rick out of your hair."

"I need to do that. Maybe I'm resisting because he keeps telling me to sign."

"You have to get beyond him controlling you, one way or the other."

I nodded. "You're right."

She reached across the table and squeezed my hand. "I've got to go, but I'll call you tomorrow."

"Thanks. You're a good friend."

She smiled, stood up and flicked her hair back, then walked out the door.

CHAPTER TWENTY-FIVE

I sat for a while after Kristen left, so many things swirling around in my head. How could I seriously be a suspect in Erin's murder? The police had to know I wouldn't have done that. Caleb and Rick had more motive than I did, and by now the police should realize Rick had been not only at the motel, but also at this coffee shop. But I wondered whether they knew about this other man that Erin had been seeing. If this mysterious man had killed her, it seemed everyone was looking in the wrong direction. Including me.

I sipped my macchiato, barely tasting it. As I did, the young woman I'd talked to the other day came by, clearing tables. I pulled out my phone and found the pictures of Caleb. Then I waved her over.

"I know I asked you this the other day," I said. "But you're sure you never saw this man in here?"

She glanced at the phone and shook her head. "I don't think so."

"You're not sure?"

I flipped through more pictures and showed her others of Caleb. She shrugged.

"What about this man?" I pointed to a picture of Rick. "You're sure he was here, arguing with the woman who was murdered?"

"Yes."

I flipped to another of Rick and Caleb, with some other people in the neighborhood standing behind them.

"You're sure you didn't mix these two guys up?"

She bent down and looked closely at the picture. "I'm not mixing them up." Then her eyes narrowed. "But that guy's been in here."

My hand touched the photo. "Him? Are you sure?" My hands grew clammy. "The night Erin – the woman – was killed?"

A head shake. "No. Other times."

"Were their conversations pleasant or did they fight?"

"Oh, no, they never fought. Not like she did with *that* guy." She tapped a finger at Rick's face, then glanced at me. "You know them?"

"Yes," I whispered.

"Huh. Well," she shrugged. "I gotta get back to work." She sauntered off.

I stared at the photo and the man she'd pointed out.

It was John Caruthers, Tiffany's husband.

The coffee I'd drunk curdled in my stomach and threatened to come up. I couldn't believe it. John and Erin had been having an affair? It seemed likely. I wondered what Tiffany knew. She acted like she had been the best of friends with Erin, right up until Erin's death. I couldn't believe Erin would do that to her friend. I exhaled loudly. This was horrible.

I stared at John's face for a while longer, then glanced across the street at the motel. I got up, my body weak, and threw my cup in the trash. Then I squared my shoulders and walked out. The warm afternoon air should've been soothing, but it only made my hands clammier. I marched across the street and into the motel office.

The clerk that I'd spoken to before was behind the counter. He glanced up, and then a small grin spread across his face.

"You keep coming in here – are you sure you don't want a room?"

I shook my head. I was still clutching my phone in my hand, and I held it up. I swiped the screen to the picture of Caleb, Rick, and John, then showed it to him.

"I know you said you didn't recognize these men, but would you look again?"

"You don't give up, do you?"

"Please help me." My voice cracked.

He chewed his lip for a moment, then looked at the phone. He picked out Rick. "He was in here sometimes."

"Anybody else?"

He studied the picture, and then his eyes flickered as he glanced at me.

"You've seen someone else, right?" I said with dread.

"Yeah." He pointed at John. "This guy."

"How often did he come in here?"

He shrugged. "Off and on for the last few months."

"Did you see him with the woman who was murdered?"

"I told you, one or the other comes in for the room, but not both."

"Has he been in here after the night the woman was found in the alley?"

"Not that I recall."

I gestured toward an old register. "What name did he use?"

He snorted. "They don't give their real names, and we hardly use the register. And they pay cash."

"Was he ever here with any other women?"

"He was always by himself." His tone was slightly exasperated.

I held up a hand. "Please, just a few more things." I got to the critical question, one I really didn't want to ask, but had to. "Was he here the night the woman was murdered?"

It was like an eternity before he answered. "I think so." He rubbed his jaw. "The two of them were together? You think he did that to her?" He jerked a thumb behind him, as if to indicate the alley where Erin's body had been found.

"I don't know," I said slowly.

"Wow."

I thanked him and walked slowly back to my car. I got in and sat behind the wheel, numb. Cars went by, but I didn't notice.

It was John. He was the other man. Unbelievable.

I needed to talk to him, but without Tiffany around. I checked the dashboard clock. 3:30. I didn't know where John worked, but I knew from watching out the window that he came home between 5:30 and 6:00. He'd still be at work now. I could go talk to him there. The problem was, I didn't know where *there* was.

Who could I ask? Caleb? I doubted that he'd even talk to me, and if he did, he'd tell Tiffany that I was asking about John, and she would warn him I was coming. I squinted my eyes, thinking. Melissa wouldn't tell me either, and I didn't think Kayla would know. I finally grimaced, then pulled out my phone and called the one person who might know, but wouldn't say anything.

"What do you want?" Rick said by way of a greeting. "Did you sign the papers?"

I ignored that. "I need something from you."

"Why would I help you?"

"Please. It's important. Where does John Caruthers work?"

"John? He works at an oil and gas company downtown."

"Where exactly?"

"It's on Larimer. Great Western Oil & Gas. What's this all about?"

"I'll tell you later."

"Okay, glad I could help." He actually sounded like he meant it.

I ended the call, got on the Internet, and found the address for Great Western Oil & Gas. It was on Larimer, near an area with lots of historic buildings that had been converted into offices and restaurants. I started my car, pulled into traffic, and headed downtown.

CHAPTER TWENTY-SIX

I found a metered parking space on Fifteenth, parked and paid, then hurried to the Graham-Clayton Building, where Great Western Oil & Gas was located on the second floor. I went up a wide set of stairs, and at the top was a glass door with the company's name on it in black letters. I went inside, and a receptionist at a glass table across from the door looked up.

"May I help you?" she asked.

"I need to speak to John Caruthers."

"Your name is?"

"Amber Aldridge."

She picked up a phone, hit a button on the console, and murmured into it. Then she hung up the receiver and said, "He'll be out in a moment, if you'd like to take a seat."

I thanked her, sat on a long white couch, and peered out the window at the building across the street. A few minutes later, John walked into the room. He looked as suave as ever.

"Amber," he said, trying for pleasantly surprised, but the tone didn't quite make it. He exuded restraint. "What's up? I never thought I'd see you down here."

"I'm sorry to bother you, but there's something–"

"Come with me," he interrupted.

He waved a hand, and I followed him down a short hall to an office that looked out on Larimer Street. The room was decorated in dark tones, with mahogany furniture and a bookcase full of golf trophies, awards, and some pictures of Tiffany and him. He sat down at a leather chair behind a huge desk, then gestured for me to sit in a wooden chair near the desk. I sank onto it, grateful I didn't have to stand any longer on my shaky legs. He sat back, trying to appear casual, but he tapped his fingertips together nervously.

"What can I do for you?" he asked.

"Tell me about you and Erin."

He blinked hard a few times. "What?"

"You and Erin were having an affair. You were with her the night she was murdered."

His gaze didn't waver, but he stayed silent. Then he suddenly stood up. "You need to go now."

I shook my head. "No. This is important."

He strode around the desk and jerked open the door. "Leave now or I'll call security." He said it loud enough that the receptionist must have heard.

I got up, walked quietly past him, and down the hall to the lobby. My cheeks burned as I crossed in front of the receptionist.

"Have a nice day," she said.

I didn't say a word as I went out the door. I dashed down the stairs and outside. Then I paused and looked back at the building. That wasn't the behavior of an innocent man. But did that mean John had had the affair, or had murdered Erin, or both? I wanted to talk to him more, but I wasn't sure now.

It was a little after four, and I decided to wait for him. Before I told Tiffany or called the police, I wanted his side of things, and I wasn't going to leave until he talked to me.

I went to my car, and waited and watched the minutes tick by. The streets grew busier as people got off work. Five o'clock came and went, but John didn't leave his building. Half an hour passed, but still no John. Then something occurred to me. What if he'd left through a back exit? I swiveled around and looked behind me, toward the back of the building. No John. I was chiding myself for not checking the building more closely when he emerged from the main entrance, crossed Larimer, and started toward Market Street.

I jumped out of my car, paused for a break in traffic, then crossed the street and ran after him. He turned onto Market, walking fast. As I drew closer, I called out his name. He whirled around, saw me, and frowned.

"I told you, I don't want to talk to you," he said.

"An innocent man doesn't act like you're acting." My voice was loud.

He stopped, then hurried toward me. I halted before I bumped into him.

"What do you know about anything?"

"Someone at the Standard Motel and at the Starbucks across the street from the motel identified you. You've been in that motel, and you were there at the same time as Erin, the night she was murdered."

"I wasn't in the Starbucks that night."

"No, but you were there other nights with her."

Fear flickered in his eyes. "I wasn't at the motel with her."

I put my hands on my hips. "Come on, you're really going to lie to me?" I grimaced. "How could you do that to your wife, and to Caleb?"

He took a step back and glanced away. Some people passed by, and he moved over and put a hand on the side of the building as if to steady himself.

"I know what you think, that I killed her, but I didn't."

"How do I know? How does *anyone* know?"

He shifted, leaned against the building, and swore. Then he bent down. "This whole thing is making me sick."

I moved closer to him. "You were with her that night."

He nodded slowly.

"You want to tell me about it?"

He coughed and stared at the sidewalk. People passed by, but neither of us noticed them.

"How long had the affair been going on?"

He straightened up and swallowed hard. "A few months," he finally said.

"Did you know she was also seeing Rick?"

"I knew that, but she was going to break it off with him."

"Don't tell me it's because the two of you were going to be together."

He jutted out his chin defiantly. "Yeah, we were. We were in love. She was going to leave Caleb and I was going to leave Tiffany. Once the divorces were final, we were going to get married."

"You really believe that?"

"It's the truth."

Somehow, I didn't think that had been Erin's plan, but what did I know?

"Does Tiffany know about your affair?"

"No," he murmured.

"You haven't told her, now that Erin's dead?"

"No, and you better not say anything."

We stared at each other for a minute, and then I moved on.

"Tell me about that night."

He bit his lip. "She had seen Rick earlier at the coffee shop. She was tired of him hassling her, and she said she told him in no uncertain terms that it was over between them, and he wasn't to bother her anymore. He got mad, I guess, but after he left, she came over to the motel. I had rented a room, and she met me there." He stopped.

"And?"

He glared at me. "Do I have to draw you a picture?"

"How long were you there together?"

"A few hours. She left around eleven, and I left shortly after that."

"Did you see where she went?"

"No."

"Where was her car?"

"She'd leave it at the shopping center the next block over."

That fit with what Detective Maddow had told me.

"Like she'd shop in that neighborhood." The sarcasm in my voice was clear.

"Better than the car being seen at the motel," he said.

"What'd you do after you left there?"

"I drove home. It was about 11:30."

The set of headlights I'd seen that night.

"That's a late night," I said. "What'd you tell Tiffany?"

He shrugged. "I had a late meeting. I do a lot. I have to wine and dine clients. She's used to it. I can be out half the night and she doesn't think anything of it."

"That doesn't help your alibi."

"Tiffany can vouch for me."

"Maybe. Did anyone at the hotel see you leave?"

"No."

"And even if someone had, you still could have driven around the block, found Erin walking to her car, and killed her."

He took in a big breath. "I didn't do it. I loved her."

"Rick said the same thing," I said.

He shrugged.

"What happened?" I pressed. "Did you have a fight with her, and when it went bad, you killed her?"

"No!" He contemplated me for a long time. "What're you going to do now?"

I pursed my lips. "I've been hearing that Erin was meeting with another man at the motel. That's you. Unless you tell me there were more men besides you and Rick."

"Erin wasn't like that."

"Uh-huh."

"What're you going to do?" he repeated.

"Tell the police about you."

"They'll think I killed her."

"They think *I* killed her," I said harshly. "But you know I didn't."

"You can't tell them about me."

"I have to."

He flew toward me. For that brief moment, no one was on the street. He grabbed me by the arm and yanked me into a nearby alley.

"What're you doing?" I gasped.

He slammed me into the side of the building and held me there.

"Don't do it," he snarled. "If you tell the police I was there, it'll ruin me. Do you know what would happen if everyone I work with, and my clients, knew I was accused of murder? It wouldn't matter that I'm innocent, it would kill my career."

"Fine," I said. I was shaking, but I tried to put on a brave front. "I won't call the police, not yet. I'm just trying to get to the bottom of this."

"You've got to believe me," he pleaded.

A man in a dark suit paused in front of the alley and stared at us. John stepped back.

"Are you okay?" the man asked me.

"Yes, I am," I said. I looked at John. "I think we're done here."

John nodded. "Don't say anything," he muttered.

I walked out of the alley. The man eyed John as I passed by him.

"You sure you're okay?" he asked me.

"Yes, thank you." I straightened my shoulders and walked down Market to Fifteenth.

The man waited a moment, then followed. I heard his footsteps, and I glanced over my shoulder and gave him a quick smile. He returned with a reassuring nod. I peered past him, but John hadn't appeared. I hurried to my car before he could follow me.

CHAPTER TWENTY-SEVEN

My hands shook as I started the car. I was so flustered that I pulled into traffic without looking around, and a horn blared behind me. I hit the brakes, and so did the car behind me. A horn blared again, and a woman flipped me off as she drove around me. I waved sheepishly and mouthed, "Sorry." Once I had an opening, I drove off, concentrating hard on the traffic around me.

I had told John I wasn't going to call the police, but that was a lie. That was the first thing I was going to do, but I didn't have Detective Maddow's card with me. I drove south out of downtown as fast as I could, but traffic was heavy, and it took a long time. I worried that John would head right home, too. Would he figure out what I was doing and try to stop me? I didn't know if he'd murdered Erin, but it was a good guess. And that would make him desperate and dangerous.

I finally reached my neighborhood. As I drove down my block, Melissa was just getting out of her car. She glared at me as I slowed down near my house. Kayla was walking along the sidewalk, pushing Talon in a stroller. She waved at me, but I barely acknowledged her as I drove into my driveway and in the garage. In the rearview mirror, I saw Kayla slow down, but I shut the garage door quickly. I didn't want to talk to her right then.

The garage door had barely closed before I ran into the kitchen. For a moment, I couldn't recall what I'd done with Maddow's card.

"The desk!" I said to no one.

I whirled around, went to the built-in desk by the refrigerator, and fished out the card from a drawer. I pulled my phone from my purse and dialed the number.

"Maddow," she said a moment later in her cool voice.

"It's Amber Aldridge."

There was a pause.

"Yes? What are you doing calling me?"

"Erin McCormick was having an affair with my neighbor, John Caruthers," I blurted out.

"Oh? And how do you know this?"

"I just talked to him and he admitted it."

"That's interesting."

"He was at the Standard Motel with her the night she was murdered."

"And how do you know this? He admitted it to you?"

"Yes. I've been trying to figure out what she was doing that night."

"I've been doing the same thing," she said wryly.

"I finally stumbled upon John."

"You just happened on this information?"

"I know you think I was involved, but I'm not. Erin is not who everyone thought she was."

"Then who was she?"

"She was having multiple affairs," I said, a little desperation in my voice. It felt as if Maddow was toying with me, and I didn't like it. "Not only with John, but … with Rick. My husband, well, soon-to-be ex-husband."

"I knew about Rick."

"I figured you did." I couldn't bring myself to say any more than that. "But she was with John shortly before she died. You need to look into that."

"John seems to have told you everything else, did he tell you that he murdered Erin, too?"

"Of course not," I said.

"So, your husband was having an affair with Erin, and the neighbor John was, too."

"Yes! What if John was jealous of her, or they got into a fight, and he killed her?"

"What if you were jealous of her because she slept with your husband, and you killed her?"

"Why would I do that? I'm about to divorce Rick."

"Who knows?"

I sucked in a breath. "Are you going to take this seriously or not?"

"I am, and I appreciate your passing along the information."

"That's it?"

"What more should I say to you?"

"I …" I stumbled for words.

"You have a nice night, Amber." She thanked me and ended the call.

I stared at the phone for a moment, then dialed Kristen. She answered right away.

"What's up?"

"I need your help."

"What's wrong?"

I told her everything, and finished with, "I can't believe Detective Maddow doesn't believe me."

"You don't know that. She's not going to let you know what she does or doesn't know. You did the right thing in calling her. And promise me you'll stay inside and keep the doors locked. We don't know for sure whether John murdered Erin, but if he did, who knows what he might do next."

"He wouldn't do anything to me here," I said. "He'd get caught."

"You can't predict what a murderer will do. You just stay safe." She sighed heavily. "I've got a dinner meeting I can't get out of, but I'm coming over right after that, and I'll spend the night."

"You don't need to do that."

"Yeah, I do. Better safe than sorry, right?"

"Right."

"It may be late before I can leave," she said, "so keep your phone by you. I'll call when I get there."

"Thanks."

"You bet, sweetie."

I ended the call, relieved that she was going to come over. I hadn't realized how scared I was until I talked to her. I didn't think John – if he was a murderer – would do anything to me tonight, but Kristen was right. No sense in taking chances.

It was after seven, but I had no appetite, so I went upstairs. I went into my bedroom and stood in front of the window. It wasn't my usual place, but I wanted to see when John came home. Or, maybe he'd stayed downtown, or he could have arrived home without my seeing him.

Dusk settled in, turning the sky into a deep blue. I didn't bother turning on any lights. The sky turned black and then the moon rose, bathing the street in silver hues. It was quiet and peaceful, everything I wasn't at that moment.

A light was on in Caleb's house, and then one went on at Melissa and Bill Lowenstein's. John and Tiffany's house stayed dark. I didn't bother to turn on my bedroom light, but stood in the dark. How many times had I done that, either waiting for Rick, or fantasizing about Caleb, wishing my life had been different? Now I was watching again, not sure whether my neighbor across the street was a murderer.

As I looked down on the block, I mulled over my conversation with John. He'd denied having anything to do with Erin's death. He – like Rick – had fallen hard for Erin. But where was John's motive? He was adamant that he hadn't killed Erin. Then he'd lost it when I said I'd go to the police. Was it just about his career and money? He must have been worried about what would happen when the police figured out he was with Erin that night. That would put anyone on edge, but especially a murderer. And he didn't have an alibi, unless he could get Tiffany to lie for him. But she might not be in the mood to do that for her cheating husband.

The street grew lighter, and headlights appeared. A dark car came down the street and slowed as it neared my house. John was home. I remembered Rick saying he'd seen a dark blue car at the motel. John's?

The car pulled into the driveway and floodlights lit up as he drove into the garage. I waited for the door to close, but instead, John suddenly appeared at the end of his car. He stood in the shadows and looked at my house.

I backed up, afraid he'd see me, even though my bedroom was dark. He stared at the house for a long time, not moving. It was creepy. I braced myself, my breath coming in shallow gasps. Then John finally turned around and disappeared into the garage. A moment later, the door closed, the floodlights shut off, and the street was dark.

I sat down in a chair in the corner, the night heavy around me. I wasn't sure what to do. John still might come after me. I wished I had a gun in the house. And yet, I didn't know whether I could shoot it at someone anyway. I was working myself into a tizzy. I needed to calm down. Kristen would be here later, and it would be okay, I kept telling myself. And John wasn't stupid enough to act rashly and get caught.

More light filled the window as another set of headlights appeared on the street. Then I heard the familiar purr of Caleb's car. I stood up and went to the window. A dark car slowed down and turned into the Caruthers's driveway.

It suddenly hit me. Tiffany's Mercedes had the same sound as Caleb's. As her car pulled into the garage and the door went down, things fell into place.

The night Erin had been murdered, I'd heard a car coming home around midnight, and then another one a while after that. I'd assumed the second car was Caleb because of the sound it had made. I'd heard it so many times as I'd watched him from the front window, that comforting sound. I didn't even think about Tiffany's car having a similar sound. John had come home right after he'd been with Erin. And Tiffany had arrived not long after that. But long enough to have seen John and Erin leave the motel, then murder her.

More things made sense.

The fight that Tiffany described to the police, supposedly between me and Erin, when she quoted me as saying, "stay away from my husband," had been between Erin and Tiffany. She wanted Erin to stay away from *her* husband. She'd made up a lie about me, using her fight with Erin to her advantage. And with that casual lie, Tiffany easily shifted the suspicions toward me, rather than at her.

And who better for Tiffany to frame than me, the woman who had a crush on Erin's husband?

The whole thing was crazy. I rubbed my hands over my face. Then, before I could change my mind, I grabbed my phone and dialed Maddow. It went straight to her voicemail. Damn!

"It may not be John," I said breathlessly. "Tiffany Caruthers may have killed Erin. Please call me back so I can explain." I ended the call, and suddenly was truly fearful. What if John was telling Tiffany about our conversation? What would she do? I needed to get out of the house, but I didn't know where to go.

Caleb. I could go to him, and explain everything. Tiffany wouldn't look for me there.

I ran downstairs and into the hallway, flicked on the overhead light, then flung open the front door.

Tiffany was standing there.

CHAPTER TWENTY-EIGHT

In Tiffany's gloved hand was a small black gun. I didn't know what make or model it was, just that it was real, and it was dangerous.

"Tiffany," I said, trying to be much more casual than I felt. "What's going on?"

She moved toward me. I stepped back into the foyer, away from her and the gun. She shut the door behind her and glared at me.

"So you figured it out."

I tried to play dumb. "I don't know what you're talking about."

Everything about her, from her ruffled shirt, to her pinched brow, and the gleam in her eyes, said crazy.

"It all would've been fine if you'd just left things alone," she said. "No one suspected me."

"I had to do something."

She nodded, a satisfied smile on her face. "Exactly. They wouldn't have been able to prove you'd done anything, though, and they would've eventually let it go. And no one would've been the wiser."

Her eyes glinted malevolently. She was on the edge.

"Why'd you do it?" I asked. Something told me to keep her talking.

"John was going to leave me to be with her." The gun wavered just a bit. "I couldn't have that." She motioned with her other hand. "I have the house, I don't have to work … it's a great life. What would happen if John ditched me? She didn't need him. She had Caleb." She swore. "She slept with everything that moved, and that still wasn't enough. She had to go after John."

"You didn't need to kill her."

She laughed. "She needed to be out of the way."

Her eyes were wild, but the gun never wavered. I bit my lip. She had no remorse about murdering Erin, and I knew right then that Tiffany was going to kill me. She'd entered the realm of the insane, and she didn't care what she was going to do, or whether it meant she'd get caught.

"Let's talk about this," I said, trying to buy a few precious minutes. "It doesn't have to be this way. I'm sure John still loves you, and you can work things out with him."

She laughed harder. "John … I don't want to talk about him."

"You and Erin were friends," I said. "I'm sure you didn't mean to do it, not to your friend."

"Ha," she spat out. "You've seen what kind of friend she could be. She already despised you because you were so … so beneath her. And then when she realized you had a crush on Caleb, she was livid."

"She didn't love him," I said softly.

She snorted. "It didn't matter. You were a threat. And why are you defending her? You know she slept with Rick, right?"

I nodded.

"And then she went after John. And who knows who else." She shook her head in disgust. "That woman deserves no sympathy. She certainly didn't care about Caleb. And look at you, going after him like you did. He was too weak to stand up to her, and never even suspected her. Why would you want someone like that?"

"Don't talk about Caleb like that," I whispered. And yet, something in her words about Caleb rang true.

"He should've stopped Erin, before she got to John."

"Why don't you run?" I said. "I haven't talked to the police about you, and as you said, they don't suspect you. You could leave the state now, head to the coast and disappear. Start a new life somewhere else."

"They'd find me."

"No, you would be okay. People do that kind of thing, and they never get caught."

She tensed up, and I knew I didn't have much time. My mind raced, trying to come up with a way to talk her out of killing me. My legs felt shaky, and I put a hand on the table.

"It's time to end this," Tiffany said.

"How're you going to do this and not get caught?" I replied. "This is crazy."

The wild look faded, and her face was deadly calm. "I'll make it look like an accident. I read enough crime novels." She held up the gun. "I got this to use on Erin. It's untraceable. But I didn't shoot her, so ..." The smile returned. "I'll use it on you."

My hand moved on the table, touching the vase that Rick had given me.

"What happened in the alley?" I asked. Keep her talking.

"I followed John one night and saw him meet Erin at that motel. That's how I knew about them." A faraway look crept into her eyes. "I followed him a lot. Sometimes he really did meet clients, but most of the time, he met her there. "I tried to get him to forget about her. I did *anything* that SOB wanted, whenever he wanted it, just like he wanted it. You know what I mean." She gave me a look. And I *did* know what she meant. "But," she continued, "he just grew more and more distant. And then one day I knew what he was thinking, that it was over between us. He was going to leave me, and I knew I had to do something about it. I got the gun, and waited for the right time. But I never seemed to catch Erin alone, or when it was dark. Until that night. I waited for her in the alley because she always went that way to her car. It was raining, but I didn't care. I'd suddenly found myself unsure of the gun, so I pocketed it. What if someone heard me shoot her? How stupid could I be? Then I saw her coming toward the alley. She had such a satisfied look on her face, and I hated her. How could she do this to me?" Her voice grew soft. "I saw a long board lying next to the dumpster, and I picked it up. I hid by the dumpster. She walked by me, and I swung the board at her. She went down and ... that was it."

She was so cold and calm, it was terrifying.

"And then I walked away. No one saw me, nobody knew. At the time I didn't really care if I got caught or not. I was so angry at Erin, and at John, that they would do this to me. But when I realized the police didn't have any idea that I did it, I figured I could place the blame on you."

"What about her purse, and her phone?"

"I took them and threw them in a dumpster on the way home. I searched her purse first. She had her cell phone, and a prepaid phone to call whoever she was meeting, that's why Caleb couldn't have found anything on her personal phone."

I moved my hand and rested it on the top of the vase. She didn't notice.

She held up the gun. "The police won't know who this belongs to. I shoot you and make it look like a suicide. You were despondent over your divorce, and upset that Caleb rejected you."

"That's not true."

She snickered. "The police believe what I say, remember?"

"John will know. What'll you do about him?"

"I'll deal with him. We're headed for divorce anyway, but I can make sure the police suspect him. His only hope will be if I provide him an alibi."

Exactly as I'd thought. She was diabolical.

The gun came up, and then she noticed my hand on the vase. "Uh-huh. Step away from that."

I swore under my breath as I moved away from the table.

"Turn around and walk slowly into the kitchen," she said.

I turned, and then I saw the hall light switch. Without hesitation, I reached out and hit it. The hall went dark. I ducked down just as a horrific bang sounded.

She'd shot at me!

I scrambled into the kitchen and around the island to the back door. Behind me, Tiffany ran into the island. Something clattered to the floor. Her gun.

I wrenched the back door open, pushed through the screen door, and ran onto the deck. The back door opened again. I'd barely made it onto the grass. I started for the side of the house, where there was a gate to the front, but another shot rang out. I scrunched down, but felt the bullet whiz by.

"Stop!"

The moon was out, and Tiffany could see me. There was no place to hide. She walked toward me and I backpedaled right into the shed.

"Now," she said as she came slowly toward me. She raised the gun.

"Tiffany, no!"

The gate rattled and a figure rushed into the yard. Tiffany turned partway around.

"Leave us alone, John."

Her voice had reached a robotic level.

"You don't need to do this, Tiffany," he said. "This is madness."

"You need to go," she replied.

He took a few steps toward her. "I've called the police. We're going to deal with this now."

"Don't take another step," she ordered.

He kept coming. She swung the gun around and fired. John gasped and fell to the ground.

"Oh my god!" I said. "You shot him!"

"Yes." She was indifferent. "And you're next."

She turned back around and took a step toward me. I moved to the side and bumped into something. The rake. I clutched it in my hand, then swung it as hard as I could at her. She lifted her arm to ward off the blow, and a shot rang out. The end of the rake hit her on the side of the head, the thick tines cracking into her skull. She groaned and crumpled to the ground. The gun fell at her side. I backed away from her, my breath coming in ragged gasps. Tiffany's legs twitched for a moment, and then she lay still.

I ran over to John. He was clutching his side, and dark liquid oozed between his fingers.

"It's okay," he said. "I ... think I'll be all right."

"I'll get an ambulance," I said. Then I realized I didn't have my phone with me. I swore.

"I shouldn't have done that to Tiffany. I loved Erin, but I didn't see what it was doing to Tiffany."

"Don't talk," I said. "I've got to get help."

"I ..." He groaned.

Then I heard sirens. The sound grew louder, headed toward our street.

He grabbed my hand. "Stay here," he said.

"I need to tell the ambulances where we are." I looked back at Tiffany. She wasn't moving. I turned back to John. "Did you know Tiffany killed Erin?"

He hesitated, then nodded. "Not at first. But Tiffany was acting so weird." He sucked in a ragged breath. "I didn't want to believe she could do anything like that, so I kept my mouth shut. And tonight, I told her about you coming to the office, and she went ballistic. I knew I had to say something to the police, but I didn't want her to know. I went upstairs to call them, and I didn't hear her leave the house. When I came downstairs and she was gone, I knew she'd come over here. Is ... she going to be okay?"

I glanced behind me again. "I don't think so," I said softly.

He bit his lip. "Oh, Tiffany."

I let go of his hand. "I'll be right back."

I got up, ran out front, and waved at the emergency vehicles. Then I wrapped my arms around myself, and shook uncontrollably.

CHAPTER TWENTY-NINE

I stood in the front window again. The sun was shining and the street was quiet. It was as if all my neighbors were too stunned by last night's events to venture out on this beautiful morning. It had been enough for them to absorb Erin's murder, but then to find out what had happened last night ... that was too much.

My gaze went to Melissa and Bill Lowenstein's, then to the McCormick house, and finally to the Carutherses' house. Tiffany's looked picturesque, as it always did. I stared at it for a long time. The old adage was true. You never knew what happened behind closed doors.

I picked up my mug of coffee from the table. My hand shook. I was tense and sick about what I'd done last night, even though I knew I'd had to. Tiffany was going to kill me, and she'd left me no other choice. That knowledge didn't make it easier. I sipped some coffee, then listened to the sound of my breathing, trying to relax. I eventually reached a point of pseudo-calm. Then I set my cup back down.

Coffee might not be the best choice right now, even though my weary body needed it.

"I should work in the garden," I said to myself. "Or ..." My voice sounded hollow in the big living room. "It's time to make a change."

But I couldn't make myself step away from the window. Looking out onto the street was comforting somehow. Then movement caught my eye. Caleb was walking down his driveway. He stopped at the end, stared at the Caruthers' house for a long minute, then started slowly along the sidewalk. He crossed the street, and I realized he was heading for my house. I backed away from the window, even though I was sure he knew I'd been looking outside. He came up the walk and rang the doorbell. I went to the foyer and opened the door.

"Hello, Amber," he said, his voice not as strong as I once thought it was. "How're you doing this morning?"

"I'll live."

He nodded slowly, then gestured past me. "Do you mind if I come in for a minute?"

"Not at all. Come in."

I stepped back and let him inside. For some reason – I wasn't sure why – I didn't ask him to sit down, so we stood in the foyer. He shifted from foot to foot, then finally made eye contact.

"I'm really sorry about everything."

I pursed my lips, then gave him a quick nod.

"It was wrong to think you had something to do with Erin's death. I should've known better."

"It's okay," I said, even though it wasn't.

"I was so mixed up about everything, and Tiffany kept pushing me, telling me that you were jealous of Erin, that you'd fought with her. She painted you in such a negative light, and I believed it." He shrugged, then repeated, "I should've known better."

"We missed a lot, about a lot of things."

"What's going on with the police?"

I sighed. "I'm waiting to hear. I told them everything last night, but they're still wrapping up the investigation."

"You acted in self-defense."

"Yes, but only John can corroborate what I said, and I don't know what he told them."

"The truth."

"I hope so."

We stood in uncomfortable silence for a moment.

"The funeral is the day after tomorrow," he said. "You're more than welcome to come."

"I appreciate that." At this point, I didn't know if I wanted to go, but I left that unsaid.

He gave me a small smile. "Maybe when this – you know, with the police and the funeral – is finished, we can go for coffee and talk about all this. I'm sure this has been hard on you."

"It's been hard on you, too."

He glanced around. "It's weird. I'm not used to being in a quiet house. Having my in-laws has helped, but it's just …" His voice trailed off.

I hesitated.

"We can just talk," he said.

"We'll see."

"Well, I'll let you go. If you need anything, just call."

"I appreciate that."

I opened the door and he headed down the sidewalk. I moved to the living room, but stayed back from the window. Caleb crossed the street and disappeared into his house. He had given me an opportunity, an opening to get to know him better. And who knew where it would lead? But I hadn't committed to anything. What was that about?

I pursed my lips, then grabbed my mug, went into my office, and opened my laptop. I got onto the Internet, found some online job postings, and began scrolling through them. Anything not to think about last night. I stared at the screen. There were several jobs that would be a good fit for me. My pulse quickened with excitement as I thought about going back to work. It was what I really wanted, what I shouldn't have given up. Not for Rick, anyway. I checked my resume, made a few changes, and applied to a few of the jobs. It felt good.

I glanced out the window as a gold car pulled into my driveway and Kristen got out. She walked swiftly toward the front door, in a rush as always. I grabbed my mug again, and had barely made it to the foyer before she flew through the door.

"How're you doing this morning?"

That was the question of the hour.

She'd come over last night while the police had been here, and she'd stayed the night. She'd had to leave for an early meeting this morning – working on a Saturday – but as she'd promised, she was back. She held up a white paper bag.

"I brought donuts. Let's go in the kitchen."

I followed her down the hall, then poured her a cup of coffee, and we sat at a small table in the breakfast nook that looked onto the back yard. I shifted away from the window, not wanting to see where Tiffany's body had lain.

"So," she said as she munched on a donut. "Talk to me."

"I'm trying not to think about things, but it's hard." I picked up a glazed donut and took a bite. It did taste good. "I don't know how things could've turned out differently, but I wish …"

She reached out and gripped my hand. "You did what you had to do."

I felt the tears coming, and I blinked hard, then took another bite.

"It'll all be okay," she said softly.

"Uh-huh."

We finished our donuts, and then each got another.

"I made some phone calls on my way over here," she went on. "The police are continuing their investigation, but I don't think you'll be charged with anything. They've talked to John at the hospital, and he corroborates your story. It was self-defense."

"He's going to be all right?"

"Yes."

I breathed a sigh of relief. "That's good news, all of it."

She let out a mirthless laugh. "It's hard to believe all that was happening, you know, with Erin and Tiffany."

I nodded.

"But you figured it out," she said. She studied me for a moment. "I think you're finally coming out of your shell. There's something to be said for that."

"I guess so."

"Hey, take some credit. You haven't been yourself since Rick left, but this is a step in the right direction. You're stronger now, not the shell of a human being you'd become."

I smiled, then took another bite of my donut. "Caleb stopped by this morning."

She eyed me suspiciously. "Oh really?"

I told her about the conversation.

"It sounds like you could pursue that, even though I don't think that's a good idea." She tipped her head. "Isn't that what you want?"

"I thought I did, but things look different now."

"Hmm."

"I applied for a few jobs this morning."

"Really?" Her eyebrows shot up.

I nodded.

"Oh." I suddenly stood up and went to the kitchen counter. I picked up some papers and brought them back to the table. I looked at them, one final time, then handed them to her. "Here."

"The divorce papers I wrote up?"

"I signed them. It's time to move on."

She took them from me, shuffled through them and looked at my signature. "You won't regret this."

I sat down. "I know."

We finished our donuts and chatted for a bit longer, then Kristen stood up.

"Will you be okay if I run a few errands? I've got to go to the grocery store and the dry cleaners, but I'll come by later."

"That'd be nice."

She took her mug to the sink, then rushed toward the front door. I followed and she gave me a long hug, then was out the door. I went back to the window and watched as she backed out of the driveway. She knew I'd be at the window, and she gave me a wave, then sped off down the street.

I stood for a minute and stared at the other houses on the block. My eyes fell on Caleb's house. There *was* an opportunity there, but I didn't want it anymore. The Caleb I thought I knew, the perfect man I'd created in my mind, didn't exist. And I wasn't sure if I wanted the quiet, passive man that he was. I wasn't sure what I did want, but it wasn't him.

I glanced around. I didn't want all this either, the house, the neighborhood, this lifestyle. It wasn't me. And it was time to move on.

With a determined nod, I turned away from the window.

Turn the page for a sample of This Doesn't Happen In The Movies, the award-winning first book in the Reed Ferguson mystery series, by Renée Pawlish.

"I want you to find my dead husband."

"Excuse me?" That was my first reaction.

"I want you to find my husband. He's dead, and I need to know where he is." She spoke in a voice one sexy note below middle C.

"Uh-huh." That was my second reaction. Really slick.

Moments before, when I saw her standing in the outer room, waiting to come into my office, I had the feeling she'd be trouble. And now, with that intro, I knew it.

"He's dead, and I need you to find him." If she wasn't tired of the repetition, I was, but I couldn't seem to get my mouth working. She sat in the cushy black leather chair on the other side of my desk, exhaling money with every sultry breath. She had beautiful blond hair with just a hint of darker color at the roots, blue eyes like a cold mountain lake, and a smile that would slay Adonis. I'd like to say that a beautiful woman couldn't influence me by her beauty alone. I'd like to say it, but I can't.

"Why didn't you come see me yesterday?" I asked. Her eyes widened in surprise. This detective misses nothing, I thought, mentally patting myself on the back. She didn't know that I'd definitely noticed her yesterday eating at a deli across the street. I had been staring out the window, and there she was.

The shoulders of her red designer jacket went up a half-inch and back down, then her full lips curled into the trace of a smile. "I came here to see you, but you were leaving for lunch. I followed you, and then I lost my nerve."

"I see you've regained it." I've never been one to place too much importance on my looks, but I suddenly wished I could run a comb through my hair, put on a nicer shirt, and splash on a little cologne. And change my eye color – hazel – boring. It sounded like someone's old, spinster aunt, not an eye color.

She nodded. "Yes. I have to find out about my husband. He's dead, I know it. I just know it." Her tone swayed as if in a cool breeze, with no hint of the desperation that should've been carried in the words.

"But he's also missing," I said in a tone bordering on flippant, as I leaned forward to unlock the desk drawer where I kept spare change, paper clips, and my favorite gold pen. Maybe writing things down would help me concentrate. But I caught a whiff of something elegant coming from her direction, and the key I was holding missed the lock by a good two inches. I hoped she didn't see my blunder. I felt my face getting warm and assumed my cheeks were turning crimson. I hoped she didn't see that either.

Perhaps I was being too glib because she glanced back toward the door as if she had mistaken my office for another. "This is the Ferguson Detective Agency? You are Reed Ferguson?"

"It is and I am." I smiled in my most assured manner, then immediately questioned what I was doing. This woman was making no sense and here I was, flirting with her like a high-school jock. I glanced behind her at the framed movie poster from the *The Big Sleep*, starring Humphrey Bogart and Lauren Bacall. It was one of my favorites, and I hung the poster in my office as a sort of inspiration. I wanted to be as cool as Bogie. I wondered what he would do right now.

She puckered pink lips at me. "I need your help."

"That's what I'm here for." Now I sounded cocky.

The pucker turned into a fully developed frown. "I'm very serious, Mr. Ferguson."

"Reed." I furrowed my brow and looked at my potential first client with as serious an expression as I could muster. I noticed for the first time that she applied her makeup a bit heavy, in an attempt to cover blemishes.

"Reed," she said. "Let me explain." Now we were getting somewhere. I found the gold pen, popped the top off it and scrounged around another drawer for a notepad. "My name is Amanda Ghering." She spoke in an even tone, bland, like she was reading a grocery list. "My husband, Peter, left on a business trip three weeks ago yesterday. He was supposed to return on Monday, but he didn't."

Today was Thursday. I wondered what she'd been doing since Monday. "Did you report this to the police?"

She raised a hand to stop me. "Please. I already have and they gave me the standard response, 'Give it some time, he'll show up.'"

That one puzzled me. The police wouldn't file a missing persons case for twenty-four hours, but after that, I was certain they would do something more. "They didn't do anything?"

"They asked me some questions, said they would make a few calls to the airlines." Amanda paused. "They were more concerned about my relationship with Peter," she said, gazing out the window behind me. The only thing she would see was an incredible view of a renovated warehouse across the street. For a brief moment, her face was flushed in as deep a sadness as I'd ever seen. Then it was gone, replaced by a foggy look when she turned back to me. "You see, Peter wasn't exactly what you'd call a faithful husband." She frowned, creating wrinkles on an otherwise perfect face. "Well, that's not completely true. He was faithful, to his libido at least. But not to our marriage." I paraphrased the last couple of sentences on the notepad. "He travels quite a bit with his company, computer consulting, so he has ample opportunity to dally. And he never tries hard to conceal what he's doing."

"Did you tell the police all of this?"

"Yes. I believe that's why they're not doing that much. That, and the fact that there appears to be no foul play, has kept them from doing little more than paperwork."

"You're afraid they're not treating his disappearance seriously."

"Exactly."

I scratched my chin with the pen. "I'd have to disagree with you about that." I didn't have much experience – okay I didn't have any experience – but in the tons of detective books I'd read and all the movies I'd seen the police would take someone of Amanda's obvious wealth with some concern. At least until she gave them a reason not to.

"They don't have the resources to track him down," she countered. "That's left up to me, which is what I'm here to do."

"And this way you also keep any nasty details private."

"Exactly."

"Why come to me?"

Amanda glanced around the sparsely furnished office and the stark white walls decorated with nothing more than movie posters, as if she were second-guessing her choice of detectives. "You came recommended. I know you're not licensed but…"

"You don't have to be in the state of Colorado," I interrupted. Anyone who wanted to could be a detective here, just hang up a sign. Hell, you didn't even need a gun. I could testify to that. Never had one, never shot one.

She waved a hand at me. "I don't care if you're licensed or not. I know your background. You come from a well-to-do family; you know when to be discreet."

I came recommended. Now that caught my curiosity. The only

thing I'd done was to help a wealthy friend of my father track down an old business partner. It was slightly dangerous but not noteworthy, and at the time I didn't have an office or a business. I had been between jobs, so I decided to pursue an old dream. I hung up a shingle to try my hand at detecting. I loved old detective novels, had read everything from Rex Stout and Dashiell Hammett to Raymond Chandler and James M. Cain. I'd watched Humphrey Bogart, William Powell, and all the classic film noir movies. I pictured myself just like those great detectives. Well, maybe not. But I was going to try.

"Who recommended me?" I asked. The list was surely small.

"A friend at my club."

"Really? Who?"

"Paul Burrows. Do you know him?"

I shook my head. "Does he know my father?" I assumed he was someone who'd heard about me helping my father's friend.

"I don't know, but Paul said you were good, and that you could use the work."

She was right about that. I lived comfortably off an inheritance from my obscenely rich grandparents, plus some smart investments I'd made over the years, so I'd never had a real career. I had always wanted to work in law enforcement, but my parents had talked me out of that. Instead, I got a law degree, flitted from job to job, and disappointed my father because I never stuck with anything. I hoped being a detective would change all that; it was something I'd always wanted to do, but my father still thought I was playing around. I needed to solve a real case to prove him wrong.

"Are you a fan of old movies?" Amanda asked, noticing the posters for the first time.

I nodded. "I like old movies, but especially detective film noir."

"Film noir?"

I pointed to a different poster on another wall of *The Maltese Falcon*, one of Bogie's most famous movies. "Movies with hard-boiled detectives, dark themes, and dark characters."

"And dark women?" Amanda said.

I kept a straight face as I gazed at Lauren Bacall. "Yeah, that too."

"I hope you're as good as Sam Spade," Amanda said.

I watched her cross one shapely leg over the other, her red wool skirt edging up her thigh. Trouble. Just like I'd thought before. I should have run out of my own office, but I didn't. I know what you're thinking, it's her beauty. No, it was what she said next that complicated things immensely.

"I'm prepared to pay whatever it takes." Saying that, she pulled a stack of bills from her purse. I crossed my arms and contemplated her. This sounded like I'd just be chasing after a philandering husband. Not exciting at all, even though I had little basis for making that assumption, other than what I'd read in books. But a voice inside my head said that making money meant it was a real job, right?

I named my daily wage, plus expenses. It was top dollar, but she didn't blink. And I had my first real case. What would my father say to that?

*****

"Let's start with you clarifying a couple of things," I said. Moments before Amanda had inked her name on a standard contract, officially making her my first client. "How do you know your husband's dead and not just missing?"

Amanda sighed. "Because he would've called me, kept in touch, and I haven't heard a word from him."

"But if he was out with someone else?"

She shook her head. "No, he always calls. He pretends things are normal. We have our routine and he always follows it. Only this time he didn't."

"But he knew?"

"That I knew?"

I nodded. She nodded. "Yes, he knew."

I resisted the urge to continue the Dr. Seuss rhyme. "So he hasn't called you, but what makes you jump to the conclusion that his not calling means he's dead?" I leaned back in my chair, tipping it up on two legs. "What if he wanted to disappear, or he's fallen in love with someone else and has run off with her?"

Amanda emitted a very unladylike snort. "Peter's not capable of love, so it's impossible for him to leave me. Not for that reason, anyway."

"Have you given him another reason to leave?"

She hesitated. "I was going to kill him."

We moved out of the realm of boring. The chair legs hit the floor hard. "Excuse me?"

"I was going to kill him," she repeated. She stared down at her hands and ticked items off on an index finger. "For the insurance money and the inheritance. Well over five million. Besides that, I would get my freedom from the farce of our marriage." She spoke matter-of-factly, as if she were detailing a cooking recipe. "I was trying to figure out a way to do it. I couldn't make it look like a suicide, because I'd lose out on the insurance money. I couldn't murder him, because I couldn't guarantee getting away with it, and I might not get any money that way either. A domestic dispute gone bad was out of the question because Peter wouldn't hit a rabid dog, let alone his wife. I was left with creating an accident. Only I never could figure out what to do. Help him lose control and drive off a snowy mountain road? Too much risk for me. Electric shock of some sort? But how could I pull that off? Poison? But with what, and how to keep it from being discovered?" Her breasts lifted and sank in a deep sigh. "I finally gave up," she said and looked me straight in the eye. "I didn't do anything."

Blurting out her plans like that intrigued me. Bogie never had it this easy. "But he's disappeared," I came back to the original point. "How do I know that you didn't have him killed?"

"Why would I hire you?"

"To make it look like you weren't involved."

She smiled. "I'm afraid that's impossible. First of all, I wouldn't know where to start. And as I said, I gave up the idea of killing him."

"Then how do you know he's dead? If he knew you wanted him dead, that's a lot of motivation not to come home."

"He didn't know anything about it."

"But you just said that he might not come home because he knew you were trying to kill him."

She emitted an exasperated sigh. "Peter never knew anything," she said again.

"How do you know?"

She spoke to me like I was the class dunce. "All Peter knew was that our marriage, and his money, were in jeopardy. When I was considering what I might do to him, I was less," she struggled to find the right words, "less than kind to him. Cold. Indifferent. He sensed that. Then I decided I was being foolish, so I resumed the game. Things were back to normal, whatever that was. He didn't have any reason not to come home."

I sat back again, feeling like I'd missed the answer to a test question. "So I'm supposed to find your presumably dead husband, whom you wanted to kill, but deny that you did, and now that he's gone, you want him back."

"Yes," she said, exasperated.

"Fine," I said.

I should've run, right then. I should've, but I didn't.

Ebook available at Amazon. Paperback available at Amazon and Barnes & Noble.

ABOUT THE AUTHOR

Renée Pawlish is the author of The Reed Ferguson mystery series, the Dewey Webb historical mystery series, *Nephilim Genesis of Evil*, The Noah Winter adventure series, *This War We're In* (middle-grade historical novel), *Take Five*, a short story collection that includes a Reed Ferguson mystery, and The *Sallie House: Exposing the Beast Within*, about a haunted house investigation in Kansas.

Renée loves to travel and has visited numerous countries around the world. She has also spent many summer days at her parents' cabin in the hills outside of Boulder, Colorado, which was the inspiration for the setting of Taylor Crossing in her novel *Nephilim*.

Visit Renée at www.reneepawlish.com.

The Reed Ferguson Mystery Series
This Doesn't Happen In The Movies
Reel Estate Rip-off
The Maltese Felon
Farewell, My Deuce
Out of the Past
Torch Scene
The Lady Who Sang High
Sweet Smell of Sucrets
The Third Fan
Back Story
Night of the Hunted
The Postman Always Brings Dice
Road Blocked
Small Town Focus
Nightmare Sally
Ace in the Hole (novella)
Walk Softly, Danger (Kindle Worlds novella)
Elvis And The Sports Card Cheat (short story)

A Gun For Hire (short story)

The Dewey Webb Mystery Series
Web of Deceit
Murder In Fashion
Secrets and Lies
Honor Among Thieves
Second Chance (short story)

The Nephilim Trilogy
Nephilim Genesis of Evil
Books Two and Three soon to be released

The Noah Winter Adventure Series
The Emerald Quest
Dive into Danger
Terror on Lake Huron
Book Four coming soon

This War We're In
Middle-grade historical fiction

Take Five
A Short Story Collection

The Sallie House: Exposing the Beast Within
Non-fiction account of a haunted house investigation in Kansas

Made in the USA
Coppell, TX
23 June 2021

57940173R00138